BLUE
SELF-PORTRAIT

BLUE
SELF-PORTRAIT

Noémi Lefebvre

Translated from the French by
Sophie Lewis

TRANSIT
BOOKS

Published by Transit Books
2301 Telegraph Avenue, Oakland, California 94612
www.transitbooks.org

Originally published in French as *L'Autoportrait bleu*
by Éditions Verticales © Éditions Gallimard, Paris, 2009

English translation © Sophie Lewis 2017
First published in English translation by Les Fugitives, London, 2017

The rights of Noémi Lefebvre and Sophie Lewis to be identified respectively
as author and translator of this work have been identified in accordance with
Section 77 of the Copyright, Designs and Patents Act 1988.

ISBN: 978-1-945492-10-5
LIBRARY OF CONGRESS CONTROL NUMBER: 2018932617

DESIGN & TYPESETTING
Justin Carder

DISTRIBUTED BY
Consortium Book Sales & Distribution
(800) 283-3572 | cbsd.com

Printed in the United States of America

9 8 7 6 5 4 3 2 1

TABLE OF CONTENTS

BLUE
SELF-PORTRAIT

THE CAPTAIN ANNOUNCED SOMETHING NO IDEA WHAT, the steward demonstrated how to breathe with the mask on and how to tie the life jacket but I didn't look up. I had exactly an hour and thirty minutes in which to switch languages. You'll have to change that way you talk, my girl, I told myself in German, in French, then in German again, then in French, as if I was my own mother. I took stock of my wounds, from head to toe, from my head hammering with the wrath of grapes, my hunched shoulders, the skitterings in my stomach, my weak knees, both right and left, to my arms and legs grown skinny and me trembling all over almost without stopping; in short I was suffering a fundamental lack of serenity despite sending out serene signals; I was practically basking in fulfillment if you went solely on appearances. If I had allowed my inner goings-on to show you'd have taken me for a cow bellowing at the moon like the time in my car when I started bellowing, moo-calling, I mean, the nocturnal call of the cow, I still wonder how I did it that night, that particular freezing one, I emitted such a horrid bovine

9

cry, there must have been something of the animal in me,
a cow on the road, a great cry between two moments of
civilization, of Zivilization, I was in simultaneous translation, now crazed down to my bony cylinders I reined in
my savage cry, channeled all my energy towards serenity
and it was working, so it appeared, no one in this plane
would have heard my terrible cry of blöde Kuh as people
call each other in Germany, stupid cow, I was translating
in simulcast, the domestic yet animal Kuh who looks for
her calf at dawn although she knows with her portion of
bovine gray cells that the calf with the number-stamped
ear will never come back because he is too lastingly not
there, goes on calling out for a day or two but ends up
buttoning her bellow, goes back to ruminating as if she
never had that calf, one calf, nor two or three or any
calf with or without a number, the animal who truly
sees the dying of each second. I had bellowed so hard
that evening that I'd frightened myself, I was so closely
aligned with the cow that I was practically in symbiosis
with nature, toe-to-toe with nature, as if between she and
I the distance had vanished, verschwunden, I translated
automatically. And now the desire to bellow seized me
again, in mid Berlin-Paris flight. You go to Venice and
you end up dying in Venice, you go to a sanatorium and
you end up with tuberculosis, one's environment has a
disproportionate impact, I observed yet again, this time
inside the plane: no matter what exactly changes around
you, wham you are completely messed up, maybe even

dead. I hadn't noticed takeoff, yet I was flying and, as I'm not the keenest breed of traveler, the mere fact of our flight could in itself have sent me into a tailspin, the altitude alone potentially enough to tip me over, though I was unaffected by this flight still my sister was. We're flying my sister said, can you feel it, we're flying! Flying has a big impact on me, every time feels as big as my first flight, I could see the effect on her but nothing for me, I said I could feel it but I couldn't; so we wouldn't get started I opened a book and got stuck in. I did my best to lose myself in my book, to become as one with the book, to think of nothing outside it, to feel nothing except what was sensed by my eyes on the paper but of course I could see myself clearly trying to forget myself and trying to become as one and dissolve myself so really I wasn't absorbed in anything, was becoming nothing and could feel nothing at all. That was a super trip my sister said, said over and over, and I replied yes, super, exceptional, I'll never forget it, she said again and I replied me neither, never. I was actually thinking never, truly never, how could I forget, and my insides were exploding noiselessly while meltwater flowed from my forehead and down my back.

Coming out of the Kaiser Café in the Sony Center, after dizzying the pianist with a flood of verbiage, I'd literally floored him by talking, I took advantage of him being German-American to clap him on the back matily as I've seen Germans do and also in old American films, though it's rarely done by women, I don't recall a woman ever doing it in an old American film, I was devastated that I'd talked so much, I talked your ear off, so so sorry, I said while clapping him on the back like a man which I'm not, like an old friend which I'm not, like an old girlfriend which I wasn't at the time when he said no, not at all, it's quite all right in his German-American accent—I must have said my bit in German and he replied in French. Ich habe zu viel gesprochen and I clap him on the back, no, not at all, it's quite all right, and he touches my arm in the German or American way to communicate friendly affection, I went on, in French now, that it was he who had taught me so, so many things, and I who it seemed was now teaching him something. I had less than nothing to teach him but it was too late, I had talked so much in my passionate, learned and over-expansive way that he must have given up somewhere along the line, actually when I began, from the first word I spoke, from the first parting of my lips and as if to compensate for my missing tooth I had already talked too much, in that passionate, learned and oh so shameless way, you cut modesty class the pianist might have said, so your mother didn't teach you much about modesty but he didn't say it, would have had he been me but the pianist and I are two separate people, he modest and I immodest, it was all coming back to me now in the plane between one cloud and the next, between nought and nought, difference condensed, the shamelessness came back to me all of a sudden, I saw myself as I am, so immodest, a fact screaming out to be recognized though it wasn't, nevertheless, doing that much screaming, neither that fact nor anything else. The passengers were reading and drinking coffees, a plane is no place for screaming, cars yes but not a plane, cars are perfect for your ordinary, personal scream, a scream of truth without obvious motive but the plane solely for un-premeditated and collective screaming with clear and present motive. Why, I wondered belatedly, couldn't I simply have sat and read my book at the Kaiser Café? and why couldn't I have had that coffee at Café Einstein two days earlier, drunk a nice coffee while leafing through the newspaper as has been done at the Einstein for centu-ries in the same relaxed and cultured manner, with the peaceful murmur of a little Mozart piano concerto that never did anyone a bad turn, why couldn't I have done that, been sitting on that chair in the Einstein without knotting up my legs as if they were venomous snakes and hunching my shoulders as if the weight of the world were upon them when here, at the Einstein, no one ever feels the world's weight on any part of them, even at the worst point in world history, unswervingly dedicated to its café reputation, and I knew it as soon as I walked in, fifteen years since I'd last been here but everything was the same so I knew it, you can't put that down to ignorance. This is the place where the whole world is reading the papers, I had told my sister you'll see, and I said it again because I found it witty, Café Einstein is a refuge from the world

which contains the whole world in its newspapers. It's
true that it's relaxing, a retirement home for those of frag-
ile constitution such as girls like me; it's arresting here and
arrest is a break from the world, I was explaining to my
sister, my best audience, security is relaxing when you're
cultured as the people in here are. Nuclear war could
break out but it wouldn't make a difference to the mood
in Café Einstein, I thought then as I'd already thought
before, but I don't know if it was with relief or irony or
indifference this time or before, we would read in the papers about the catastrophic effects of a nuclear war on
the people of Berlin, completely wiped out, every single
neighborhood annihilated, the utter destruction of
Charlottenburg, the total elimination of the Europa
Center and the demolishment into terminal smithereens
of the Gedächtniskirche, the memorial church, I translated to myself, memorial of what, memorial not of rout
but of nought, the obliteration of all the beautiful grand
houses on Kurfürstenstrasse and of all its residents in a
great sweep of destruction would make front page news
right up to the Einstein's front door—and all this listening
peacefully to that sweet little Mozart piano concerto.
Some guy could perfectly well walk in wearing a suicide
belt and blow the buffet to kingdom come right there in
the main salon shouting Allahu Akhbar and we'd be
reading about it in the papers while smoking the odd
cigarette and listening with half an ear to the light, in-
offensive concerto as Mozart in the background always

has been, for as long as background music has been around. Why couldn't I content myself with flicking through *die Welt*, a man of culture as all the men here are, a discreet and peace-loving man of culture who twiddles the silver spoon in his coffee without knotting up his limbs like snakes and smokes moderately, in no way like a trooper; why did I have to terrorize the pianist from the word go with my ideas about everything? You have ideas about everything, the pianist could have said but he didn't say it; sometimes it's good to keep schtum, he could have said, so interrupting, with this common-sense remark, the unquenchable stream of observations and ingenious associations that flowed from me, each new idea more striking, subtle, singular and wondrous than the last, the pianist thus arresting this verbal invasion, as voluminous as it was shapeless, barbarity versus culture at the Café Einstein, where ideas flow noiselessly and only achieve their impact in the silence of the written and their profundity in the meditation of print. I'd have done better to read *die Welt* like any other habitué and better to enjoy the concerto floating around me while leafing through the paper in that relaxed, cultured way typical of the place, I could've it wouldn't have been hard, if I'd only followed the natural inclination of culture as ushered on by the establishment, retreat and arrest-cure, I wouldn't right now be exploding on the inside in European airspace, between nought and nought, indifference on all sides. Instead of making the most of that hallowed arena reputed the most conducive to culture, I was considering it now in the plane, therefore much too late, in shame, deep shame, I re-coiled my legs like venomous snakes and hunched my shoulders, what's more I'd blitzed the pianist with a blizzard of shameless data in the purest tradition of girls without any self-control, inflicting on him the worst tortures of the Inquisition with my ill-educated habit of breaking the rules of conversation, which I'd never learned but I could at least have aped, the ape copies man better than I do I was thinking, catching sight of my misplaced girl's head in the Café Einstein mirror; nothing of the ape to be seen there, apery as limitation and imitation as a guarantee of decorum, the decorous ape missing from the mirror where the extra-to-requirements indecorous girl sees herself as she truly is, what are you doing here, far from the ape, what is it you're really after, leaping from branch to branch in front of the mirror like an ape-imitator, the inhumanity of the animal aping not man but ape, in instinctive imitation I leapt at any old straw. But what is it you're really after? the pianist finally asked, blushing at my volleys of apery, my sister aping her ape for one act and I aping my sister for act two, we, my sister and I the Ape Inquisition and the pianist begging for mercy, how I ever came to this, interrogating an innocent pianist in the hot-seat of a popular intellectual café I don't know, what I do know is that nothing will ever make it not have happened. I had to interrogate him, I had to trample barbarously upon the oh-so-French rules of conversation that I ought to have learned from Madame de Staël who I always refused to read, the quality of Madame de Staël's conversation in the Prussian salons a model of restraint and French good taste but I just had to interrogate him in the most obnoxious way, I tried out my inquisition on the pianist who had come here specially to see me, the venue his choice, here precisely in all Berlin, to see me, he had chosen this perfect spot to promote from the start a peaceful, reassuring and cultured climate between us, tailor-made for our conversation and its disposition, instead of which he found himself hauled in for interrogation by an entirely shameless girl descended from apes, accompanied by a sister clearly fruit of the same tree and with hardly more moral compass than the first girl as far as he could tell.

One more piece of luck: I didn't explain to the pianist how to play the piano, it was touch and go, I told myself later in the plane, it was a close-run thing, I could very well have done it, I'm perfectly capable, I know I'm capable of explaining the art of the well-tempered keyboard to a pianist as if I myself were a virtuoso. I don't know anything about music, I'm sitting in front of a virtuoso pianist and explaining exactly how your fingers should rest on the keys, *see* what I'm capable of. *I'm* explaining to *him* how to do it, as if the virtuoso pianist were just waiting for me all along to show him the best way to go about it at last, as if he was going to be filled with wonder at all the little pianistic techniques that I would

generously furnish him with so he could improve his playing and become even more virtuosic thanks to me. I truly
am capable of leading a masterclass for a great pianist
of worldwide renown. Of explaining (I can just see myself) how one ought to tackle the second movement of
Beethoven's Concerto in C major, for example, the opening attack, the crisp yet simultaneously resonant C chord
and, in sweeping overview, on the generosity—I could
hear myself in full flow—discoursing upon the generosity
in Beethoven as if this were possible, and then upon the
detail, a marginally lighter touch here, a little more color
there; I would quite have expected the pianist ultimately
to modify his interpretation of the second movement and
to follow these little tips freely given by me, who cannot
play the piano and know nothing about Beethoven. A
piece of luck I narrowly squeaked out of that.

Two days later, leaving the Kaiser Café where I had
once again all but spelled out to the virtuoso pianist how
to handle his piano, a stroke of luck that I'd stopped myself just in time, I uttered my notorious Ich habe zu viel
gesprochen for it was true, I had said too much, so much
too much that I had to proclaim this brand-new truth
the very moment it occurred to me; my noble pianist: no,
not at all, it's quite all right, he sweetly replied, warmly
replied, even though it wasn't fine, not only not fine but
catastrophic, so catastrophic as to be irreparable, besides
I didn't repair anything but on the contrary promptly
went and dug myself in deeper: of course I had to

interrupt again, when I had only just said Ich habe zu viel
gesprochen, I didn't pause and count to ten, not to ten
nor to any lesser number, I didn't count at all; I just had to
go on and on in the underground car park when he, our
poor pianist, was already and indeed for some time had
been, broken, kaput, as they say, in fact just five minutes
after stepping inside the Kaiser Café he'd already begun
to yawn, ten minutes in was out of commission and quite
kaput, and yet here we are in the underground car park
and I'm picking on his car, I have to make some comment
about his car being unworthy of a world-class pianist, as
if all that I'd said before in the Kaiser Café hadn't been
appalling, about music in general and the pianist's playing
in particular even though I haven't the first notion about
music in general, and as for the pianist's playing in particular here I go even now critiquing it from every angle,
not only the music performed by the pianist but also that
composed by the composer, the pianist being both pianist
and composer, I am a pianist first and foremost and yet
foremost and first of all I am a composer, the pianist said
one day to all within earshot, indeed the pianist did have
a talent for composing that not every pianist is blessed
with—and the composer a pianistic virtuosity to which
few composers may lay claim, both gifts united in a single
person, in the perfect bodily and spiritual harmony that
alone could justify the general and nevertheless exceptional title of musician; I am, above all a musician, the
pianist said, it isn't my profession but my condition, yet in

spite of his condition I held back a mere hair's breadth away from explaining to the pianist how to play the piano and to the composer how to compose. In the car park right now, I'm inspecting his vehicle, inside and out, the state of the bodywork, the ergonometry of the seats, I've estimated its resale value and underestimated all other values, sat in there ready to ride shotgun though minus the gun, broadcasting my observations about his car, unworthy as it was of a world-class pianist, it's no good, however clearly I see it coming I always end up slagging off anyone and everyone precisely when tête à tête with a very particular someone, I brazenly sabotage all chance of a future as if I didn't know that what's said is said, retraction is out of the question, it is definitively too late.

It's the same every time. Every time I vow I won't let it happen again and every time it happens. If I was the pianist, I'm sure I would have got on my nerves, a girl who has just apologized for talking too much and then motormouths slap into another clanger: my car, to boot. You can't know what kind of bond unites a driver and his car, impossible at first sighting to grasp the often complex and very personal rapport between driver and car; the nature of the car says something about its driver and the driver likewise about the car, any car salesman will recognize the highly sensitive nature of this complex relationship but I in my bulletproof girlhood, unsullied by all mechanical considerations and without regard for the mechanic's expertise, boldly I attack, no quarter given, the subject of his car upon which it turns out that the pianist attaches immense importance to the old banger and loves it truly and feels that he and it are only whole when they're together. He drives his car on ex-GDR roads, on these roads of the former republic that are still complete chaos, he crosses the still deeply sorrowful countryside, this once-upon-a-time republic still effectively lying fallow and as good as medieval, a pure pleasure, super-real elation, oh the deep, deep joy of the driver driving free, independent, wealthy with all the possibilities, why should he give a damn about notions of relativity and me telling him without the least respect for his perhaps terribly personal and intimate relationship with his dreadful old banger that God alone knows one can't go round in such an old rust-bucket when one is a pianist and a world-class one at that. He's obliged to accept it, the appellation world-class pianist, simply forced to swallow the irony in that title and to face the fact that for me, Miss Bulletproof herself, knowing nothing of the dynamics of pleasure, a car like his must be the object of jocularity, even ridicule, while for him nothing of the sort, reigning Miss Immortal, I trample anti-commercial values without restraint and deny the possibility of any attachment so deep, so powerful, so authentic, to this car and no other, as to be practically in the pianist's DNA, when the same pianist was just the other week driving this very banger (though world-class in his eyes) through the fields and copses of that erstwhile republic, heading for Neuhardenberg

Castle, in other words, he was touring about the open country, joyously driving in the sub-sublime and frozen landscape of the Brandenburg backwoods, at the far edge of reunited Germany and a mere ten unlucky kilometers from Poland, a Brandenburg castle then a Prussian one then Nazi then Communist and then returned to its heirs and state-subsidized into a space of high unified German culture, the superbly restored castle of Neuhardenberg as described in the leaflet, the hallowed place to which the pianist was driving at the wheel of that altogether world-class car the company of which alone could make him whole, to see the exhibition "Music and the Third Reich."

Invited to the private view, he was clean-shaven and his hair brushed but not over-brushed, the nonchalance of his hairstyle a style but nonetheless not an affectation, knowing as the pianist did the difference between style and affectation not only in the artistry of his playing, in particular, but also in his art of life, in general, the art of living with hair at ease and the art of playing with moderate pedal-usage, was driving on those still-chaotic roads and through the relatively medieval countryside, that smooth, masterful driving, not overusing the pedals, as the driver so the pianist, both gauging their pedaling just right, I gauge admirably the pianist was thinking of traversing fields and woods, gauging away, driving to-wards the cultural castle, he was not going to the private view for private viewing but intending to see the show without ulterior motive, had heard about the exhibition long before receiving the invitation, had received the invitation but long before receiving it already decided to visit the Brandenburgian castle of Neuhardenberg, was regardless of the invitation au fait with the music of the Third Reich, had practically no expectations of the private view, expected neither primary nor secondary benefits, had never expected more of private views than that he would not linger over them but he did have expectations of the exhibition; from the private view of course he would gain nothing more than the grease of hands shaken and presentations on autopilot but from the exhibition something, an affirmation, why not even a discovery, had indeed discovered Schoenberg's Blue Self-Portrait, seen the majority of Schoenberg's paintings, got to know the musician and also the painter. Most composers know nothing of Schoenberg's approach to painting nor do most painters know much about his style of composition. The pianist had seen most of the self-portraits, yet had never before seen the Blue Self-Portrait, so stopped before that blue, felt the anxiety and chill, the awareness of time and negative space folding into itself, sought some affirmation that he knew would be pointless, bent over the case that held Schoenberg's letter. He had peered at the letter and read it three or four times from the bottom up, starting with the signature which he knew and recognized, it was a humdrum letter to the Reich's culture minister, Schoenberg pleading with

the culture minister to recognize his music's value to the
nation, imploring one last time but too late, had in reality
already said fuck off to the Nazis, fuck off face-to-face,
Scheisse! Schoenberg's face versus the Nazis' face—that
Schoenberg had balls, the pianist reflected as indeed he
did every time he thought about Schoenberg, thought to
himself while standing there facing the Blue Self-Portrait,
to have balls or not to have them, the blue's affront to the
radiant sky and its chortling countryside, Scheisse to the
Nazis long before they were marching through Munich.
Look at that look, thought the pianist, anti-Nazi the look
and anti-Nazi the portrait's blue, Schoenberg's expression promised nothing positive for the art of the future,
conveyed an anxiety for the future, looked far beyond any
definition of the work of art or of the future; the pianist
weighed Schoenberg's solitude and Schoenberg's solitary
conscience flaunted in advance: an insult to the national-
socialist ethic, and it was with the pure, burning joy of
having deepened his conscience, as pianist both composer and musician, thanks to this proof of Schoenberg's
courage as a painter displayed in the Neuhardenberg
castle, that the pianist got in his car and drove back to
Berlin, his heart punching his ribs, that he found, perhaps
precisely in his own little car, puttering along the zoned-
out roads of the Brandenburg countryside, a sparkling
new, completely original and perfectly formed line of
music, shaping there at the wheel and in anticipation the
perfection of man in his time and man in the idea. The

idea is indeed beautiful but it's nothing without time and time is nothing without the idea; as a musician he had a sense of time as tempo, driving around in the pre-Polish countryside, the sense of this musical idea in time, dazzled by his insight, perceived the limits of his idea outside time, had to stop the car in order to get his brand-new melody down on paper, sitting in his car pulled over on the hard shoulder, right there he wrote down the melody. Thinking back to the pianist's car made me feel sick, my knees went weak and my head was burning, I could have passed it off as airsickness but really it was shame, plain and simple, and by association of shames I recalled driving the pianist-composer-driver right round the bend by making him go up and down Neue Kanstrasse three times because I could no longer find the entrance to my Polish hostel, and my shameometer measured a new record with that devastating memory, my soles were damp, my temples throbbing and my eyes squeezed shut in aged penitent-nun style—which comes straight from my education—remembering the pianist's exasperation after the third of our three back-and-forths, his deep sigh, his ever more visible and ever less restrained impatience for us to be done, um Gottes Willen, by the grace of God Schluss! Will this never end! I heard him, the irritation in his gritted teeth, I burned with shame as I pictured once more the pianist's hands clamped rigid on the wheel, the pianist's exasperation you had to see his clenched jaw, the pianist was wondering given apparent circumstances and who could blame him when this interminable evening would be over and at what hour he might finally go home to bed not to dream but to sleep that peaceful, silent, restorative sleep without visions that would allow him to hope for a new day just like all the other new days required for the equilibrium of a pianist-composer, a new day shaped by the essential practice that the pianist relied on to play the piano and the composer to compose.

I dived into my book with ridiculous zeal, I gulped down a dozen of Thomas Mann's letters to Theodor W Adorno and a dozen of Theodor W Adorno's to Thomas Mann, thinking it's never too late to learn and staking everything on general knowledge and on literature in particular as if I could understand anything of the very lofty adumbrations of the one and of the equally lofty cogitations of the other, the other being just as singular as the one and the one as particular as the other, as if, through this correspondence about returning and in the language of Goethe which was beginning to escape me in great swathes and to dissolve into airspace, I might hope to grasp the most piddling portion of meaning in the pianist's music, to accede to the pianist's interpretation, knowing as he does better than anyone Adorno by heart and Mann by heart, and able, at the drop of a hat to give a public lecture on music in literature or on literature in music, when my sister said for the umpteenth time "I just love planes." My sister just loves planes, she has flown over Madagascar in a plane, seen Johannesburg by plane,

Venice by plane, she's been in love with an aviator, fallen head over heels for the aviator's plane and when you're in love it's forever, she had her eyes glued to the porthole, admiring our plane's wing or, more precisely, its air brakes, saying it was crazy to think that one fine day some guy had invented the air brake, she said that was a real boy thing to invent the air brake, as if girls all had other fish to fry, lucky we had men to invent the air brake I thought, otherwise the only way out of here would be by parachute and parachutes also needed men to invent them. I used to know a para a time ago. He used to vacuum between the sheets, slept with a revolver under his pillow and played chess against himself. He had dumbbells and resistance bands and used to rub petrol into his hair so he wouldn't go bald. He had a set of identical paratrooper's shirts with epaulets and a set of stripy vests, also identical; a pile of indistinguishable shirts, a pile of vests: that was his wardrobe. Later on I copied him with the vests, I had a stash of them which I built up one by one, gradually, a vest for every jilting, quite soon I had a fair number, I had compiled my anti-marital wardrobe, having everything the same does not encourage connubiality, I revealed to my sister who has no inside knowledge of the subject but extensive acquaintance from the outside, my stack of vests was my para uniform, Debout les paras il est temps d's'en aller sur la route au pas cadencé, he would sing Debout les paras, il est temps de sauter sur notre Patrie bien-aimée, had come to my parents' house to whisk me away, had arrived at the parental home by sky like a true para, cooee, here I am, from time to time he would throw himself at my feet and say, hands clasped in supplication, "I doan' deserve ya" in his over-egged manner that confirmed my belief in very little indeed despite my religious education. Why do I remember the para now, perhaps so I can forget the pianist a minute, it makes a change but not much of one in the end, my identi-kitted para and pianist, para uniform and the pianist's not so different, the para's fatigues and those of the pianist comparable in every respect, the pianist dressed as a pianist and the para as a para, both of them dressed equally comme il faut for civvy street and for combat, the pianist's civvies equivalent to the para's, the pianist as much in awkward camouflage as the para in their respective civvies, I noted the consistency of get-up that marked the pianist as belonging to one classification and the para to another without making either one or other truly classifiable, each man first of all himself and not the other but each of them equally standard-issue, the one adapted to the international concert stage and the other to the French-speaking lands of Africa, the pianist at heart a fish out of water in francophone Africa and the para a shadow of himself on that stage I mean on his knees hands clasped I doan' deserve ya, the pianist frankly looking rather silly out of uniform, that's why I made that observation about his get-up as if this pianist's mufti were my business, why I pointed out his civvy style, it's funny seeing you like this,

I said without counting to ten, nine or any number at all, I said I actually said it without a moment's pause for thought it's funny to see you in civvies, das ist komisch, said it without even counting to one, dropped that word komisch about his get-up just as I had once also found the para's wardrobe of identical shirts and identical vests thoroughly komisch, it seems I haven't made much progress between him and him, however different they were I had to spout my observation unsupported by any prior observing, why did I bring in the para? it was my sister and planes, my sister and her beloved air brakes, a fine masculine invention my sister gushed, and I thought she would have loved personally to have been the inventor of the air brake, seeing how she watched them rise and sink, why didn't she invent the air brake, I suppose that comes down to her education. Thinking about my sister's education triggered inside me, that is in my deepest and most true self, the muffled, heart-rending cry of a cow, a cow calling to her calf suffocating in silence. Not that my sister is poorly educated, at the end of the day her education isn't as disastrous as all that, but it's because of mine, my education, which was give or take very little the same as hers, and thinking about my own education has me plumbing the depths of my own identity. I think about it very rarely but that's still a good deal too often and I think a good deal more often about my sister's education, almost every time I see my sister, not—once again—that she was mis-educated, there are many worse educations than my sister's, but because I know that education like no one else since it was practically the same as my own and because I often catch myself attributing her behaviors to the fallout of her education—which is a mistake for, unlike me, my sister has always been ineducable. That's where I'd got to: doing my best not to get hung up on my sister's failed education and my own successful one, when the plane swerved to the left, well to what I felt might be a left for I've never managed to acquire any certainty as to right and left not in the general sense but in the specific field of spatial scenarios, and there in the porthole, thanks to that sinister swerve, appeared the Wannsee.

I'd recognize it anywhere, you can forget trying it on with me about the Wannsee, I know it like the back of my hand, no other stretch of water seen from above can match the shape of the great Wannsee with her Peacock Island and her outlying lakes, why the clouds parted at the precise instant that the plane swerved to its supposed left so as to reveal the Wannsee I have no idea, I'd thought we were already much further from Berlin but we were still only flying over the Wannsee. And seeing it appear all at once like that socked me yet another attack of acute interior bellowing, I bellowed as hard as I could without outward expression, all the while projecting perfect serenity, pinpointed the Wannsee's beach, bovine bellow, the Berliners bathing in the summer-blue water, those renowned Berlin family picnics with baguettes and Berlin camembert and Berlin Coca-Cola, beneath trees lining

that beach of sand imported from the North Sea, warm
water rippled by the completely naked swimmers who've
been the majority for more than a century, Berliners in
their birthday suits, in fact, doing gymnastic moves on the
imported sand, after practicing their sidestroke and their
German crawl, reputedly so dynamic and powerful, were
hopping about on the artificial beach in the buff, touching their left hands to their right feet and right hands to
their left feet, but as for the Wannsee Conference I hadn't
the first notion; the pianist has always known exactly what
to think about it, he comprehends the substance of the
word Wannsee, has no need to be reminded about the
conference nor what was decided on the 20th of January
1942, the conference date is branded on the pianist's
brain, never flies out of his pianist's head while in mine
occupying only a tiny and un-synched mental broom
cupboard; the 20th of January is my sister's birthday nevertheless that never reminds me of 20th January 1942,
every 20th of January I think of my sister's birthday, a
date which fatally recalls my own approaching birthday
and vile time that keeps on passing but not once on that
date have I thought I am wishing my sister a happy birthday on the Wannsee Conference; for the pianist the date
of that conference is, should a single date be called for,
the only one to remember, no other date is more signifi-
cant than that 20th of January 1942, not for him but for
the whole of humanity, as he tells not absolutely everyone
but he does tell anyone who'll listen, he knows who was

there and why on that twentieth day in January of that year, 1942, who was sitting around the table, sitting and playing their part in the decision, knows the name of each of the participants though I don't. I spotted the Wannsee from my porthole but instead of remembering first of all the 20th of January 1942, I thought first of the Berliners who go to bathe there every summer since they brought in that fine sand from the North Sea shores, of the Berliners stretched out on that artificial beach chatting about the weather and love and the fine Berlin lifestyle without worrying again and again over Heydrich whose father was a composer and director of the conservatorium, both one and the other and who had given his son the worst of bad educations, the pianist said pointedly more than once, a bastard of a dad will make scum of his son, educated him in such a way that one day, that notorious day of my sister's birthday whose date I remembered only out by a few years, his son along with his pal Goering, yes Goering was his pal, one day he organized a conference for his friends. The pianist cannot play at all nor the composer compose without recalling that conference on the Wannsee, and Heydrich: the name is not only familiar to him but this name, Heydrich, is on his mind every moment of the day, forgetting a single Heydrich, father or son, would have immediate consequences for his interpretation of Beethoven and of Liszt, the pianist said to whoever would listen, immediate consequences for his composition and for everything else, you can't play any of

that romantic, so-called classical music as if the Heydrichs
had not existed, he would say giving his angelic smile
before launching into Beethoven, without letting up
would explain in his polite and respectful manner to the
Auditorium audience which was there to listen to classical
music and not to hear a pianist saying that to play
Beethoven you must know not only Beethoven but also
the Heydrichs, not only Heydrich the son but Heydrich
the father too, the composer, der Komponist with a big
K, a second-rate capital-letter composer nonetheless a
craftsman of German music, you do follow my meaning,
as director of the conservatorium, the pianist explained
to the girl who was keen to listen, and thus director of
musical minds, and thus instructor of young people with
bright futures such as Germany was mass-producing at
the time, instructor to the musical youth that would only,
from one day to the next, turn into Hitler Youth, verstehst
du? She did understand, the pianist saw in the girl's eyes,
the training of musical consciences means nothing to
anyone but for this girl it does, the pianist thought observing her eyes, this girl who of youth and musicianship, of
the ravages of music upon youth and of those of youth
upon music, had no historical knowledge but who knew,
how could she know, the girl's eyes now, where to put
himself in their light, he wished he'd not brought up the
Heydrichs, wished he'd spoken neither of father nor son,
thought he should have given up peddling his 20th
January 1942 from one girl to the next but each time he

catches himself banging on about that day, for the pianist discussion of 20th January 1942 is the prior condition for any relationship, but its inevitable end he knows from experience, still each time whips out his pet date and each time destroys the relationship, girls in good health fleeing one after the other or delicate girls dropping like ninepins, one or the other, but this one not fleeing or dropping, the pianist sees, flights and drops he's seen a thousand variants, but not with her, this girl who crosses and uncrosses her legs, the Heydrichs father and son don't finish her off, rather they bring the girl and the pianist so, so close together, each word on the Heydrichs from the pianist's mouth could equally have come from the girl's mouth, so naturally that the pianist would like to kiss and lay her down and hold her tight against him until all fundamental differences have been effaced; I should have remembered about the 20th of January 1942 when I caught sight of the Wannsee then saw it disappear again in the space of a heartbeat, I don't know how I could see that water and not think first if not of the father at least of the son, I did think of them but too late, the mistake once again irreparable. The spontaneity of my nonthinking about Heydrich the younger pierced me like a dagger-thrust, the kind that makes warmongers regret war, once again I was ashamed too late as is always the case with me and shame, a belated shame with this devastating effect on my physical condition, and on that of my morale as well as my physique, so terribly moral and much too belated as ever when it comes to me and

morality. Moral spontaneity should be learned as young
as possible, a flaw in my education I thought, here I go
again complaining about my education, a complaint
that's good for nothing but to justify a lack of moral spontaneity; that the two Heydrichs, the Nazi friend of
Goering and the Nazi composer and conservatorium director should have zero moral spontaneity: that is what
permitted the Wannsee Conference; that this education
was catastrophic for Heydrich's personal development
and for humanity: that's what the Wannsee Conference
proved, and even if Heydrich had said something, pointless to expect a single word from Heydrich, however I've
strained to hear it, the pianist said, I've never heard that
one word: Entschuldigung. Thanks would not have made
much difference, made absolutely no difference for the
millions of cadavers foreseen by the younger Heydrich
and his friends at the Wannsee of whom Goering was his
closest pal, as badly educated as Heydrich, the education
of Goering the man is far removed from the education of
man in general, which is a construction of man in the
idea, the pianist said one day at a conference at Humboldt
University, Humboldt's education is like that of Schiller
an exemplary education, an ideal education, die
Erziehung des Menschen, that of Goering was not and
all's done that's done. The plane's wing rose again, I dived
into a letter from Adorno, I recalled the pianist's saying
that if Adorno had been attended to Heydrich would
have stayed put in the place he belonged, he'd explained
to the Auditorium audience before beginning

the concerto, in his place as Heydrich's son dramatically educated by his composer father, not only but also purveyor of a collective musical future and director of the Conservatorium, in his place as a murderer, and had Mann not written to Adorno we would have to read the correspondence between the Heydrichs father and son, the conservatorium director and the murderer, that's what we'd have to read, the pianist said to the Auditorium audience which was losing patience, there not for history but for classical music, with no wish to rehash the old tale, what's done is done, the impatience of the Auditorium audience which wanted to hear Beethoven's music not listen to Beethoven's howl, let themselves be moved by Beethoven's music without knowing if Beethoven's bust had ever been chiseled for Hitler and if Beethoven was played at Theresienstadt, I began to sweat so copiously that I had to take a handkerchief from my pocket and wipe my face and hands, my back was soaked, I had caught the Wannsee fever, I knew this was no air-sickness but rather the sight of water, of that water, of the Wannsee, which resembles no other waterway seen from above. You go to Venice and end up dying of cholera, you go to a sanatorium and contract tuberculosis, you catch sight of the Wannsee and burn with fever, step into the Kaiser Café and you'll die of shame.

At the Kaiser Café, there before the pianist, I ordered a Berliner, I looked relaxed, sitting in a club chair by the window, resolved not to knot my legs like snakes nor scrunch my shoulders up, I must say that after my Café Einstein experience I was defensive. You're terrifying him with your wired body language, my sister said, think what you'd be like in a massage parlor or a Turkish bath! I couldn't see myself in a Turkish bath, I've never frequented baths of any stripe or massage parlors, hairdressers are torture enough, I said to my sister, letting myself be shampooed, then snipped and styled and sent to the dryer to wait under that hood and finished off with hair spray, it destroys me every time, pamper myself at the hairdresser? not on your nelly, beneath this hair I resist hairdressing so hard that instead of feeling better leaving than when I went in, I feel worse, to be honest, I come out of there each time with a stranger's head on my shoulders, no relation to the rest of me, interior and exterior no longer connected, capillary alienation as re-self-estrangement, die Entfremdung beim Friseur, I translated, you're mixing everything up said my sister, you confuse getting your hair done with looking after yourself but they're two separate things, my sister knows what I'm like, looking after yourself means aligning your mind to be in tune with your body, my sister sometimes comes out with this kind of thing. I could already picture the healthy mind in a healthy body, it was the end and the means brought together but which one to begin with, I asked myself there in the Kaiser Café. First I tried to focus on the healthy body and started smoking as if it was my last smoke in this life, all smokers believe they're smoking their last smoke more than they ever used to and until they feel sick. Thomas Mann and Theodor W Adorno were in my bag, I was counting on them for the healthy mind, between them those two would get me over my DTs, Thomas Mann had good reason to worry about culture and literature, Theodor W Adorno his own reasons to fear the worst for music and philosophy, here in the Kaiser in this cozy ambiance I had no real reason to worry, I was trying to keep perspective by switching between the two and in order not to be found waiting for the pianist while I waited for him, when in he came.

The pianist's entrance is always a big moment, I had expected this moment to be a big one and I wasn't disappointed. He was admirably himself, pianist and composer and himself all at once, did not appear as the pianist making his entrance but entered, made his entrance without ostentation or affectation or complication, nor in any other manner but simply and authentically without care for authenticity, not trying to make an authentic entrance and not presenting himself as a pianist entering but simply came in. The simplicity of the pianist's entrance struck me like a bullseye in my club chair, already I was under his spell before he'd said a single word and without his having to play a single note, in any case there wasn't a piano in the Kaiser Café and he wasn't there for a recital, wasn't dressed as a pianist but in everyday things, was not wearing his pianist's black polo-neck or his standard black trousers with the crease at the front or his black polished recital shoes, presented himself au naturel but not naked, in casuals, I instantly noticed the pianist's lack of elegance, elegant at Café Einstein but not at the Kaiser, the pianist quite as awkward and under-cover as the para in his civvies, the pianist komisch in civvies, laidback like any friend coming by for a coffee in the company of any lady friend, as one does now and then when one is well brought up and this pianist was that, had no need of any special education to make him well brought up without, for all that, having to comply with the requirements of collective happiness. Not a trace of collective happiness in our pianist. Nothing in his eyes to make you think that the pianist might at some time or another have been burdened by the quest or the realization of this collective happiness, no trace of happiness in this smiling, warm and friendly person, sitting in the club chair beside mine, I began to shiver from head to toe, couldn't stop shivering although it wasn't cold and I didn't have the flu, but was trembling like a sick sheep. From cow to sheep my bestiary is domestic, I realized to my annoyance, I should have preferred a wild animal without a pack on its back, I could just see myself galloping across the steppe or the pampas or the taiga and gamboling unwittingly like a savage without a stitch on, skin and bones nothing more, what a stupid sick Dolly I am, the pianist has noticed, he has seen the sheep's shivering but made no comment either agreeable or disagreeable, he has counted to ten unlike others such as myself, ordered a blended rather than a single malt, topped up to the brim with water and ice, so straight away, despite my sheepish and shaky state, I allowed myself to use the whisky to break his ice. Why I started with the whisky I'll never know but what I do know is that's where I started and nothing now can make it so I didn't. He'd hardly ordered his tall blended whisky on the rocks when I pointed out, in the thoughtless way I've made my own, that he was a real American to be drinking a thing like that; why I said that I've no idea however I turn it around in my head, perhaps because I couldn't make myself wait, sat like a sheep in my club chair, for him to begin the conversation himself, perhaps because as soon as he arrived I noticed a slight malaise about the pianist, and by way of reassurance could muster only an old-fashioned bit of chaffing, perhaps a way of establishing our relationship on a level of frank camaraderie from the outset. If I'd been able to show off my frank camaraderie by taking a spin round the table while sat backwards astride my chair like those imbecile Nazis of course I'd have done it, I thought there in the plane, I could see myself singing one of those Nazi hymns to the glory of comradeship, schmettern die hellen Fanfaren, I established my relationship with the pianist thoroughly indifferent to collective happiness on this re-pugnant platform, calling him American in a stupid and frankly Nazi-comradeish fashion despite knowing noth-ing at all about his personal feelings towards America. You never know what kind of bond an American may have with America, one not only American but also German, not only German but also a pianist, that not only but moreover a composer, not only him but actually anyone at all with America, it's a mystery this bond any Tom or Dick can have with America, the pianist's America was measured out in bourbon, topped up with water and chilled with ice, that was the only way to appreciate whisky in its American incarnation, which is what I was missing, I was sticking with my well-known good taste, not innate but belatedly acquired, in the context of an apparently successful marriage which had led me to encounter though not necessarily recognize all kinds of whiskys, single and pure malts, and to despise fans of blended whisky, those drinkers being not enlightened enthusiasts but a lower class of consumers, as conceded by all true enthusiasts distinguished by their refusal of admixture, consumption combines while good taste defines, this is what I'd learned in the context of my marriage, my objective then: success founded on the theoretical knowledge of whisky, I therefore pursued the single-mindedness particular to good taste which cannot be learned for lack of a particular upbringing. These were my prejudices around taste, acquired belatedly and still channeling my judgment in accordance with conventions whose universally relative nature I didn't always understand, I judged without considering the pianist's capacity to judge which had enabled him serenely to sip his tall blended whisky on the rocks without in any way snapping back at this my anti-American sarcasm of the lowest kind, the most questionable sarcasm given the knee-jerk anti-Americanism that the pianist was always condemning and which I'd never meant to be part of, in which I was participating despite myself, which I made no attempt to resist: pro-Americanism would have been equally poorly received, the pianist has never been pro-American, has never supported America for America's sake nor America versus the rest of the world, he has more than once taken a stand against America but without anti-Americanism either knee-jerk or of any other kind, ordering a blended whisky on the rocks was not a pro-American decision and called for no further anti-American critique, yet I criticized the pianist's choice without first taking a deep breath and counting to ten or any other number, criticism he thought uncalled-for, being first and foremost a pianist-composer well up on America, better informed than he is hard to find. The pianist's bond with blended whisky was in some way loaded, so I gathered from the nervy way the pianist had placed his order, as if it were quite a complex order and called for lengthy explanation to the Kaiser's waiter, who it seemed did not serve tall blended whiskys on the rocks every day, the way he snatched up the glass and made the ice swirl inside it. Doubtless the pianist felt a personal bond with blended whisky, not in the way an alcoholic effectively fosters a personal bond with her drink, the pianist, I'd observed right from the start, has nothing remotely alcoholic about him, nothing could be further removed from the pianist than alcoholism, since our first encounter he'd behaved in that naturally unalcoholic manner typical not of teetotalers, for to be dry one must once have drunk, I mean drunk the way an alcoholic drinks, teetotalism is quite as excessive as alcoholism, one high-flying alcoholic used to say who knew what he was talking about. I knew an alcoholic, he used to practice moderation in his abstinence and overdid nothing else; he'd disabused me by stealth, shooting down anything that moved, he was a crack marksman, taught me to aim and to fire into the crowd, he would shoot at point-blank range till none were left, till Auslöschung and would drink moderately till he could drink no more, would prep himself the night before for the last drink of the day to come, unfailingly downed propped upright till first light and would hold forth upon significances, philosophizing about the world, understanding the earth's tendency to spin as his world tilted and the deep meaning of everything in the depths of the bottle, with his lubricated ideas resisted non-lubricated ideas which express nothing definitively true only half-truths for the alcoholic to denounce. Denouncing the world's half-truths by means of unarguable alcoholic truths was the alcoholic's ceaseless work, it's my job as an alcoholic, he would say, wetting his ever-thirsty whistle, never missed the chance to do his job whatever the working conditions, he was that reliable with work, never put off even when it was obviously a good deal too much for one man alone. The para used to drop from the sky and skip right over the facts, swinging from his parachute he could see the army's colorful lies in Africa's outline while the alcoholic was penetrating the quintessence of the world and analyzing that quintessence which no one would ever see from a parachute, explaining how bodies fall, the free-fall of inertial bodies and Africa's free-fall down the woozy truth of the world's luge, truth lies not in the leap but in the slide, it's in the full but not the empty; at the Kaiser Café the pianist was neither between heaven and earth nor between one drink and the next, simply keeping up his unalcoholic bond with blended whisky, an intimate and precious connection, perhaps even more intimate and precious than the pianist's bond with his car, a relationship one doesn't enter into just like that, in open comradeship, but that remains for ever mystical and personal.

So, drinking his tall blended whisky on the rocks in the Neuhardenberg castle's restaurant, he waited, flanked by the black trees of three months of winter, for something to come and pluck him from this solitude which meant nothing to him, solitude often mattered to him, now and then he'd say I need solitude, would think I need it, solitude would come at his summons, on summoning it he would remain with it standing behind the wall listening to the noise of his contemporaries, could hear the noise from behind that wall better than anywhere else, sometimes he would go looking, crossing the Tiergarten on foot, beneath the striding angel, protected by the angel and whatever the weather, for solitude before the fall, would find in the garden, beneath the angel and following the path, the wall he needed for composing, on the path would be shot down by a firing squad and pictured himself falling, face-down in the dust thick with his head's blood, after which he could walk on again, at a rapid pace, does he know how to walk any way other than as if between airports, listening out with just one ear, he could hear the brand-new sounds of the brand-new year, the end of the crows and the cuckoos' début, when he thought of it though he rarely thought of it, he would set the new sounds to his walking tempo, considered the tempo, of the music not the walking, although walking and music are often associated, could hear the cuckoo, its insecure third dipping a little towards the fourth, so little it was barely, the random spacing of the cuckoo's call, the uncalculated length of the silence between each call, he was measuring the times by his steps, three steps, two, then seven, then two, four, then three, circling around Neuhardenberg the still-dominant crows, perched on the black trees and the wrong solitude, he knew that this solitude did nothing for him, drinking his tall blended whisky on the rocks, alone and more than alone, the birds are no help, made the birds vanish, off you vanish now, more solitary than ever without them, leaving the exhibition so perfectly explicit as to the effects of collective happiness, his morale fatally punctured by the display of works from the times of collective happiness: those joyous, glowing, Aryan children singing songs of happiness; pink-cheeked, broad-hipped seed-sowers sowing joy and good health; and the sunlit landscapes of peasant labor, he was at the same time resolved to suffer no more of collective happiness, of the exhibition would retain only the Blue Self-Portrait, thought he glimpsed in the darkness of the estate's trees something of nature resisting nature, like a natural idea of resistance. The pianist's fingers practicing in mid-air, the pianist's technique in practice on the fabric of his jacket, the pianist's technique in counterpoint to nature, he grew impatient as if waiting for someone, Lord above um Gottes Willen I need someone to talk naturally about nature without giving in to the natural temptation quite naturally to love nature, it must be possible, on leaving the display of collective happiness, to find refuge in some unexplored region of nature in not its natural but its savage state, not admired but brutish, not beautiful but pre-Polish. He had looked for the girl in Neuhardenberg Castle, distractedly looked but not seen her. He would have liked to bump into the girl at the exhibition but she wasn't there, he would have liked, yet hadn't gone there in order to bump into her either, didn't exactly have views on the girl nor hopes regarding her, had never looked to have any privileged relationship with her but now, over his topped-up whisky would rather have liked a girl and even that particular girl, precisely her, that one, why not, the girl laid up on rocks of ice, savored by every part of his tongue, he drove out the thought, had thought it only once but that day no, didn't want, had pictured her laid out only once but at Neuhardenberg Castle balked, wanted to discuss the exhibition, exchange a few thoughts on music and the Third Reich, discuss Schoenberg perhaps or Eisler or Brecht or Theresienstadt or the resistance to collective happiness put up by all artists classed as degenerate and persecuted by happiness even in their nightmares, with that girl he'd have had no need to explain or comment or define or defend his idea which was not a vision of the world but a counter-vision, she would have understood how he'd seen the exhibition and how he'd been changed by what he'd seen, yes: changed, not amazed or shocked or surprised, she'd have understood the mood in which he was leaving, she yes understood perfectly for she'd have seen the exhibition how it was possible to see it and absolutely not in the way it was impossible and forbidden to see it, no need to show her, that girl, how to see the exhibition nor to make her comprehend the Nazis' musical perversion. He was able at the drop of a hat to point out the alienation that music achieved, the cul-de-sac of it, the musical decay it demanded, to whoever would listen, he was ready to explain over and over, but for the girl no point, not getting hung up on these everyday obscenities, exchanging something other than harmony and something quite other than musical sentiment, she would spontaneously have kept

well away from harmony and sentiments and would instantly have seen the impossibility of all 'poetic' poetry
without his having to explain anything at all to her about
poets, wouldn't simply have grasped the impossibility but
would have positioned herself entirely outside that poetic
musical emotion, would, that girl, have been the ideal
partner to take to the exhibition. But she wasn't there.
The pianist had been alone with his thoughts about dead
poetry and music's abolition, had come out broken as a
person by a barren and devastating solitude, hands grip-
ping the glass and gaze lost in his tall whisky. He was not
however, gaze in his glass, there in the Neuhardenberg
castle's restaurant, alone in the true sense of the word, his
companion was right there, entirely pleasant company,
the ideal accompaniment in fact, the very one for him,
conducive to creativity for which you need serenity and
calm and mental tranquility and for which what you really
don't need is complications; a habit, this accompaniment,
an habitual accompaniment, the pianist might have been
thinking, relieved in the end not to have bumped into the
girl yet at the same time not altogether, for though he
really didn't want complications he did rather want them
too, didn't want the girl but did want her too, felt incapable of talking about the music but was also dying to give it
a good talking-about, one would never say anything about
Theresienstadt but something must be said, impossible to
say anything to the usual accompaniment but impossible
not to and most of all not to hear the accompaniment

talk about Theresienstadt in terms both polished from the verb to polish and acceptable from the verb to accept, discussing Theresienstadt in terms initially inadequate and finally insulting and destructive. The black trees speak more eloquently of Theresienstadt than my usual accompaniment, thought the pianist, sucking the peatiness around his tongue, staring at the black trees outside, and being so implicated in the sombre nature of the coda to a Brandenburg winter was an even greater comfort to him than Schoenberg's Blue Self-Portrait in and of itself, a self-portrait that he hung unthinkingly in the black branches whose musical significance he understood and whose palette of winter tones he found precisely those of the park at Neuhardenberg. The gloomy palette of the Brandenburgian winter added nothing to the painting; this direct connection between gloomy nature and the painting was an entirely personal fantasy, Schoenberg had painted his portrait without the black trees and the black trees themselves were self-sufficient, independent of Schoenberg.

Nonetheless, he hung the Blue Self-Portrait in the here and now of the Brandenburgian countryside, as if this was the only thing to do at this precise moment: bring together the living memory of Schoenberg as captured in the painting and the deathly presence of Brandenburgian nature, conversely bring together still and temporary life with the natural memory of Schoenberg captured in paint. Thus might the pianist have drunk his tall blended whisky on the rocks, that afternoon at the Neuhardenberg castle, in such circumstances, back in his car unworthy of a world-class pianist, slightly lubricated by the whisky and by the black trees and by Schoenberg and everything at once, inspired by each of the three elements of this serendipitous composition, he had invented an entirely original musical phrase which he'd had to scrawl down as fast as he could, a phrase that had nothing in common with standard musical phrases but sounded more like the rupture of musical phrases, the decomposition of the very principle of the phrase, a creation without precedent, a prodigious idea, a countering phrase such as he'd never dreamed of creating because, until this moment, he had attained neither the happy chance of this composition nor the car so conducive to the creative impulse, nor the negative solitude followed by a positive solitude, all come together in the ideal conjunction, the girl's absence and missing the girl, then Schoenberg, then the blended whisky and lastly Schoenberg's affinity with the black trees, he must have pulled his car up just like this in the wintry forest, in haste to scribble down the brand-new idea for a counter-phrase, written under the admiring gaze of his usual accompaniment who guessed at the supernatural and metaphysical and divine inspiration in this frenzied unrestrained fixing of music upon staves, thus she stood, the accompaniment, in a deferential and somewhat stupid silence.

At the Kaiser Café, though I'd already put the

disastrous experience at Café Einstein behind me, I nonetheless tossed out my witticism about American atavism,
as if a blended whisky on the rocks had anything to do
with nationality, anything to do with the culture of collective happiness in general and the culture of collective
American happiness in particular, even though as soon as
he walked in the pianist had made it clear that he was not
and never would be lumbered with any collective happiness, neither American nor German nor of any other
country, but that he was on the contrary impervious to
happiness, in the same manner as Schoenberg of whose
music I'd only ever heard a few notes, in passing and besides without intending to hear any Schoenberg, in the
manner of Theodor W Adorno though I've not yet read
one of his books and whose letters I was just now beginning, in the plane and without hope of return, alongside
Thomas Mann whom I'd not read before either except by
accident and without meaning to, not him in particular.
My sister was deep in the Berlin guide, looking up what
she'd seen and what she hadn't seen, thrilled to have seen
the sights she had and that she still had those to see that
she hadn't. We'll have to go back my sister said, of course
we'll go back, said it over and over, I agreed, we'll have to.
It's a done deal my sister said, I raised her a gold-plated
deal, I thought yes, of course, how could we not, I looked
for another tissue to mop up my capital and dorsal dripping, in other words my general dripping due to poor
adaptation to the pressurized environment. The Wannsee

was already far below and behind us, we must be flying over lands intensively cultivated for collective sustenance, I feigned serenity and admired the exterior effect, for a girl I'm pretty tough, I thought to myself in the plane, projecting such serene serenity, couldn't get over seeing myself so at ease, practically meadow-grazing certainly not bellowing like a cow whose calf has been kidnapped, only her poor bovine maternal feelings left to nurse, the one doesn't eliminate the other, to moo herself to death and nobody there to answer. So evidently at ease I was reading these legendary letters from Adorno to Mann and vice versa while my sister, eyes riveted on the air brakes, was telling me tales of great pilots, of masculine might and airborne derring-do, my sister elated by the takeoff, fascinated by the simple fact of having left the earth in order to fly, simply leaving Earth behind and fly-ing, said my sister, it makes me go loopy when I think about it, just that, to leave the Earth and see it from the porthole, to see it and not be there, suddenly simply not be there! The porthole and my sister formed one cyclops eye above the world while beneath us genuine German cows with no national consciousness were grazing on German grass no more aware than the cows of its own roots, oblivious cows grazing which is to say tearing up the verdure and leaving the roots, you see Friesians in Normandy, Salers cattle in Limousin and Bavarians in Switzerland, cow here or elsewhere the fate is always the same, the cry of the cow when baby calf has gone, one day, two days she calls for baby then stop, and me above everything also in flight but without the joy of the airborne, Adorno and Mann on my knees and my knees ever shakier, it was too late, what's said is said, I still and always have to say too much as I said to the pianist, Ich habe zu viel gesprochen, clapping him on the back and he, not at all, not in the least, it's quite all right, yet weary of listening to me and frankly fed up with me, desperate really for me to go to bed so he too could go to bed and this evening might at last be over. He had many things to do the next day, many the next day and the next week and all these things were being jeopardized by a single evening the absurd prolongation of which was incompatible with the good condition required to practice piano in the morning and to compose in the afternoon, seeing him yawn and look at his watch and yawn again I understood only too late, what's done is done nothing will ever change anything, I've breached the pianist's night with a truly scandalous nonchalance and yet I know this tendency of mine. You don't care my mother-in-law said in the era of my actual marriage soon over but not then yet altogether, I was on the tennis court with my mother-in-law, I no longer remember why I'd ended up playing a game with her that day, I so resistant to sport in general and tennis in particular, the problem is you don't care my mother-in-law had said, who played tennis, had played tennis always, since childhood, and won hundreds of matches, who hated losing, who ran for every ball and would come to

the net twice in a rally if she possibly could, picked up on
my not-caring just when I thought I was all energy in action, when I could have sworn on my sister's life that I too
had that killer drive to win, I had the tennis bug, that I too
was one hundred percent committed—you had to be
with my mother-in-law for your partner and in sporting
spirit—to the cause of tennis, my mother-in-law put her
finger on this not-caring in me, the demon inside her
son's enchantress, while I was focused body and soul on
dashing headlong after the ball I was laid bare by my
mother-in-law who had a definition of not-caring, I'm
wasting my time, she'd announced, you are making me
waste my time which was the precise truth, I was imposing on the time of a mother-in-law who hadn't much to
spare, not-caring requires imposing on other people's
time, I saw it there on the tennis court, not taking other
people's time seriously is the effect of an inclination not to
play games properly. That she should be so sensitive to
not-caring I put down to her life story, it was due to her
childhood and nothing else, she'd been a girl guide, I reflected on the court and again on the plane, not-caring is
reviled by the girl guides of France but also by the World
Association of Girl Guides as it is by all youth movements
who sing beneath the stars, go camping and for healthy
walks, guiding is the opposite of not-caring, as a young
girl guide in France you learn to banish all not-caring
from your life, to believe in what you do, to believe in activity in general and sporting activity in particular, as a

girl guide one believes in the value of activity as part of collective action and in sport as collective sport, in singing for the sake of singing together; one has, in girl guiding, direct and compulsory experience of happiness through activity and singing popular songs, so the pianist could have said but didn't have to for he hadn't had to take a stance on questions of scouts and guides or on any youth movement, having had nothing to do with youth movements at any level. Even the para was less scout than the Scouts, had one day got the giggles over his parachute. We can't know the precise moment my para jumped without due heed but it was somewhere over Chad, whistling his para's song all at once he'd seen the funny side of the words and falling from a great height viewed his situation with quite new eyes but not my mother-in-law, she'd never fallen from a height, had in truth never fallen from either high or low or anywhere having never been too high nor too low nor anywhere but always precisely somewhere in the right place tempered by that characteristically well-tempered temperament borne of her early years in happiness training, a fresh-air childhood whatever the weather. Hence for my mother-in-law my not-caring at tennis was an intolerable disposition typical of girls like me, an inexcusable attitude towards sport and towards life in the sense of living, joyously singing life, a fine life in the fresh air and lived collectively as life can be from a certain point of view, the viewpoint of youth movements. I didn't hit a single ball, I invariably dashed too late, I was sweating and breathless and excelling myself as best I could playing tennis, applied myself to running to and fro, hopping from foot to foot and executing little jumps on the spot while staring hard at my mother-in-law then the ball then my mother-in-law then the ball, believing I was playing tennis with every sinew and with all the conviction I could muster, when my mother-in-law discovered the root cause of everything, revealed to me who I really was, made me analyze my case, set me at last squarely before my true self, which is above all made up, I am obliged to admit, of an unmistakable plain-as-day not-caring, not-caring such as one rarely encounters, as natural to me as breathing and to all purposes, then, a deep-seated handicap. This not-caring prevents me from living normally, speaking normally, eating normally, sleeping normally, walking normally, running normally, from playing sport normally, from understanding normally what my bones consist of, from measuring the seriousness of my own body, the substance of my own body, my body's malleability, my body's presence, it was as if I didn't have a body I thought as I ran to and fro across the tennis court, winding myself and missing the ball with an impressive frequency that visibly irritated my opponent, a frequency of misses that would indeed have irritated any tennis-player who was actually playing tennis, not in the carefree manner I always affected, I couldn't see how to rid myself of a not-caring so inimical to tennis, how to be straightforwardly myself without any further agenda as if my self were in fact made up of this not-caring that my mother-in-law had noticed, noticed as has been stated in me, and the deplorable ideological and behavioral outcome. Enough of my mother-in-law now, I admonished myself in the plane, no matter that she thinks this or that of not-caring in general or of mine in particular, what difference does it make since I finished with her along with that marriage at first seemingly successful but ultimately a failure, due praise to my mother-in-law for putting her finger on the weakness in my character, which I always remember too late, when it's done it's done. If I thought more often and constructively about that game of tennis, I'd learn my lesson and I'd try to modify my principles and the behavior that flows from them but I almost never think about it except much too late. I think about it but only post-fallout. I coiled my legs up like snakes and hunched, I plunged into the letters. I read the letters but couldn't understand them. I could understand the words but not the letters, yet I was trying to understand in order to get over my not-caring but the not-caring was stopping me from understanding, understanding without caring is not truly understanding and faking understanding is not understanding, I needed not only to get over but to disavow this aspect of my character, to engage directly and without ulterior motive, but I had legions of ulterior motives, they were floating about above the letters, turning over on themselves and all pointing more or less directly towards the pianist, dancing too around that encounter in the Kaiser Café which hadn't even gone on that long, during which nothing ground-breaking or life-changing had been said but which had certainly been life-changing. In the end, nothing definitively life-changing had been said, yet from the start, in the environment of that unremarkable place, something had made all my verbal posturing as pointless as it was pathetic, a consistency in missing the ball, it was this unremarkable environment and I in that environment, the patient, generous pianist had granted me a second serving, ordered another Berliner for me, but while I was sweeping forearm over forehead before launching into a fresh conversational bout, he picked up Mann and Adorno's correspondence, which I had set down on the table, opened and skimmed through it, taking in news first of one then of the other he wasn't listening to my news, to my brand-new news he preferred the old news of Mann and Adorno, Mann's health and Adorno's analyses, Mann's birthday and Adorno's holiday, the pianist was simultaneously worried for Mann and happy for Adorno while I was relaying news of my day, a day that held no interest for the pianist, a day lost among other days, a necessary step no deeper than the usefulness of a pause. This lost time is not dead time, staying here is not about waiting but imagining, don't think of this empty time as a time to be filled, musical time like a painter's frame, a musical frame is not there to be filled up, take away the frame, pop out the picture, the painting at once within time and outside its bars, the pianist had hung Schoenberg's painting among the black trees and broken through the framework of negativity, then composed an original musical phrase in the Brandenburg forests, a brand-new antiphrase while his accompaniment for the day maintained a reverential and passably stupid silence as it often goes with reverence but ultimately perhaps a beneficial silence, productive and positive, the silence and the accompaniment's reverence an essential climate for the transformation of a musical intention into a compositional act, the antiphrase a monody perhaps or a recitative but expressionless, the sentence that says nothing, a cold shade, the cold shade in a recitative, the blue face, the painting's blue but far and scattered as if suspended, the painting in the branches, the monodic line unaffected by the crows' spasmodic cawing, ad libitum crows in peaked black uniform, three tones of the twelve, the call of birds obliged to spend their lives circling over cemeteries and denuded trees, to each naked tree a definitive bed and the individual, himself blue, who knows his own end and does not waver—my relationship with Schoenberg is changing the pianist realized. Understanding not the musician but the painter Schoenberg first of all, understanding for the first time first the painter in Schoenberg and then through the painter the musician, I'm evolving, evolving! the pianist realized on witnessing the sheer miracle written by his own hand. He had often felt Schoenberg's influence, who can resist Schoenberg, the

pianist had pondered, if not Schoenberg himself?
Schoenberg had, the pianist reminisced, held him in his
arms and kissed him as he must have held Berg and
Webern before him and any number of disciples German
and American, he had called him my little one my baby,
just as he had called Berg and Webern my little one my
baby, then as with Berg and Webern before him, had
called him my son and wished this son a fair wind, like a
father, the pianist imagined, good luck my dear son a father would say, go, explore, the father orders the son,
leave the studio behind, you don't teach an artist his art,
Schoenberg had said, the habit can be learned but not
the art, I am not a craftsman, you're no apprentice, I have
nothing more to teach you that can be learned, I've done
a little exploring but so little, said this father, what the
hell, when I'm gone ahoy the next Flood, to play
Beethoven without Schoenberg is impossible, Liszt without Schoenberg impossible, but to play Beethoven and
Liszt like Schoenberg hopeless, Schoenberg said in his
Viennese accent, it's quite simply not possible, in our
times, to play those two as if it were not our times, the pianist watched his times flow by and his brand-new musical
phrase counter-phrase itself without counterfeit. The
muttering of my contemporaries is my raw musical material said the pianist rereading his brand-new phrase, my
contemporaries' memories are also my raw material, the
accompaniment laid a hand on his right knee, a soft and
gentle hand, barely a pressure, my relationship with

Schoenberg is a musical relationship not only musical but memorial, the accompaniment contemplated the superb profile, not only memorial but moral, the accompaniment loved this profile, for having said the word memorial like that, the word moral, that's beautiful murmured the accompaniment, almost added Ich liebe dich but kept quiet so as not to disturb.

I disturb, I've never done other than disturb, I disturbed the pianist just like I disturbed a whole pack of people who nevertheless were quite well disposed to me, as I once disturbed my mother-in-law, I remember, once is enough and nothing could ever repair that one occasion which led to my original doubt as to my readiness for collective happiness, despite my mother-in-law being well disposed towards me that day, so well disposed that she had welcomed me into the privileged circle of her tennis partners, though I had already warned her of my inabilities. I'm warning you I don't know how to play, I'd told my mother-in-law but she stuff and nonsense, would stand for no gainsaying, displayed that admirable educational determination, I now know for certain, born of the girl-guiding spirit, she believed in my sporting future, in sporting futures in general therefore in mine without concern for particularities, had put her money on me as a participant in the outdoor, sporting life. She would ultimately dedicate and waste her time attempting to draw me into a tennis match in which I too wished to believe body and soul just to please her, all in all a foregone finish, without any result and losses all the way. I would have believed in anything with every inch of body and soul just to please my mother-in-law now I think about it but it's a lost cause, pleasing my mother-in-law is something anyone can do, the smallest attention is enough to make her day, no need to bend over backwards to touch my mother-in-law's heart, a small gesture of gratitude, a little thank you now and then she doesn't ask for more, not bending over backwards for her has always been the rule, flowers she won't have 'em, gushing no thank you, birthday cards and courtesy visits, all this fuss over politeness is unnecessary and even inimical to my mother-in-law's tranquility, she detests arse-lickers above all, she has often said it to the general company, that such and such was an arse-licker and she hated that. Actually it was enough not to disturb her quietude with disquiet and everything would go perfectly well, I realized though too late that something, a factor, an unknown thing in me was resisting the quietude required for my mother-in-law's quiet happiness, not that I'm an unquiet person, I am not often disquieted, all in all I'm disquieted a good deal too little in fact, would do better to be disquieted more often, it's actually a personality trait, I'm never disquieted even when it's serious. Nothing's serious for you, I've often heard that when objectively everything was serious, in those days when I was more or less living in anticipation of a para's jump bringing him down right over the family home while my sister, for her part, preferred to jump out by the window and make her getaway in a midwinter night to go and see the sea, hand me my violin, my sister'd said, I'm taking the violin to the sea and don't you go snitching on me, don't say a word to Maman or to Papa, what could be more of a blast than going to the seaside in winter with my violin, my sister exulted reaching out to receive her violin case as if it were a rugby ball, you see it's easy to run away with a violin and off she went on foot unilaterally, my sister's audacity and Papa's face in the pallid early hours, Maman's distress so upsetting to see though comforting her It's not so bad, Maman, was all I could think of to say, which wasn't in the least reassuring but actually made things worse, Maman's distress and Papa's face, nothing next to the distress caused by this inability to recognize the serious during my increasingly disastrous marriage, this truth about myself would indeed condemn my apparently successful marriage to the most complete disaster, by dint of my unconcern I concerned others more and more, a girl as concerning as me is probably hard to find, I concern as a matter of course and that's why I'm disturbing, I said to my sister in the plane which flew on straight ahead. You don't disturb anyone replied my sister who knows far better than I the truth about myself, my sister can at any moment tell the truth about me for she knows me better than anyone, she knows the entire truth about me without having to labor the disagreeable truths, she's no need to do annual accounts for my truths, doesn't total truths about me to complete a picture of my person, she has never trapped me between unpleasant truths, yet she can at any time tell me any truth about myself without ever being wrong, that's my sister for you. You don't disturb at all, really not at all, from your first cry you refused to cry out loud so as not to disturb you were already not disturbing, I remember, the day you first cried you refused to cry aloud, Maman worried about your breathing you spent so long not crying, so many times Maman begged you to cry to be sure you were breathing but you wouldn't, after that first cry that you refused to cry you became obsessed with not disturbing and you pursued your refusal of personal expression while I cried the whole time and had tantrums and stamped my feet and disturbed everybody, anyone would think you practically didn't exist, if you disturb it's more by default, the floor's yours when it comes to disturbing my sister said, you can express your presence in a much more striking way without anyone being disturbed by your crying. I know I told my sister but morally I ought to concern myself a little, I ought to show some consideration, I lack consideration living like this without disquiet, I ought to disquiet myself in life because a moral life is always disquieting nevertheless if you think about it. Morally you have nothing to worry about my sister replied and took a Brötchen out of her bag, eat please, it's teatime.

Talking about my moral life is rather ridiculous, the

pianist had said to whoever'd listen, to talk of my moral life is absurd but not to talk about it is impossible, how then to talk about my moral existence without endangering my existence, my morale and the both of them together, he often wondered. "The conviction that I have written nothing I should be ashamed of forms the foundation of my moral existence," Schoenberg had said on the 31st of March 1931 on Radio Berlin, he'd publicly referred to the moral life, radiophonically refused the collective morals of musical happiness and reaffirmed the individual morality of the composer, could have enjoyed applause but could not compose for applause, bore solitude better than shame, had chosen between shame and solitude, would reap no benefits from nor have any share in the collective happiness of which he must have been ashamed. After reading Schoenberg's letter to the Reich's culture minister, the pianist had gone back to the Blue Self-Portrait intending to examine the portrait's blue, had registered the blue's chill negativity, had taken a few steps back because of the negativity, this reflex move allowing into his field of vision a screen on which was unfolding a scene at once musical and fashionable, political and musical, Nazi and fashionable. He had only to see the director of the Reich Music Institute at the piano, that old Cavalier à la Rose gazed at by Nazi couples swimming in musical felicity, and Schoenberg's Blue Self-Portrait in the background with no audience and swimming in nothing, to be brutally plunged into that negative solitude as if he'd been rubbed out. At the restaurant in Neuhardenberg Castle he had then imbibed in his blended whisky the courage he needed to refuse applause, had hung Schoenberg's painting among the black trees in the park, refreshed his musical memory among those trees and begun to imagine the possibility of a brand-new original musical phrase, the music not collectively prepared-for but music that was personal, unheard by any before, a composition of resistance for which the pianist-composer would never have to blush.

Still, had the girl been there he'd have been able to talk to her, just talk, no need to explain but so as not to be silent, without having to reveal his personal moral code, the moral code of a composer in difficult times, he might have felt better in the company of the girl who perfectly understood the question of compositional morals, who knew about it not through musical experience but as if by magic, understood the necessity for a personal composi-tional moral code without any connection to the public mores of collective happiness, he would simply have felt all right with the girl no need to explain what to think about Schoenberg or about black trees or about music, she would have been there and they would at last have begun to explore the territories of the present, they'd have been there together in the untrod reaches of the present. The future wouldn't yet have been at issue and the girl would have known it, she'd have realized the im-possibility of discussing the future and of course would not have pushed the pianist to conceive the art of the future in this conversation, the contrary rather, would like him have persisted in anticipating nothing, she would have crossed her legs and uncrossed them unthinkingly the way this girl always does. The first time she'd already crossed and uncrossed, he had noticed, not all girls do that with their legs, some do others don't, and among those who cross and uncross many do it in a womanly manner, others in no manner at all but imitating others' manners and more's the pity, yet others cross and uncross in hopes of hiding more or less of one leg beneath the other, the less lovely beneath the more lovely, change their minds about which is less lovely and hide the suddenly less lovely more lovely one beneath the suddenly more lovely less lovely one, then give up when they realize that each of their legs is as lovely as the other, in other words they're equally ugly, too short or too fat the girls generally think, even if in fact neither too this nor too that, and end up looking actually quite fat or short, they've obsessed so much. Crossing and uncrossing the girl would have known exactly how to react, phrase after phrase always this presence of mind, she'd have done nothing more than understand the pianist not as a mother nor as a friend nor as a sister but as if by magic, would have smiled at the pianist, would have smiled sweetly and running her hand through her hair and twisting a lock round her finger and untwisting it would have shown none of the well-meaning comprehension of a mother or brother or friend but a comprehension incomprehensible if not by magic. She'd have crossed and uncrossed her legs, would have listened to the pianist without traditional insufferable feminine decorum and he'd have been troubled, as he'd been the first time, by the non-feminine understanding of this very feminine girl and indeed, he decided now as he drove through the forests of Brandenburg, again thinking about the girl though he hadn't meant to think of her again, this non-feminine understanding of hers is the most seductive thing about the girl, about any girl actually, an understanding kind of girl hardly ever attractive but a girl who understands like this girl understands, in that non-feminine or rather a-feminine even as it were counter-feminine way, everything that's most disturbing, had the girl understood the pianist with that banal decorum he'd have had no wish to chance on her again here at the exhibition, no, her indecorum, that's what he'd have liked to come across, as if by chance in front of Schoenberg's Blue Self-Portrait, if not in the restaurant that's where she'd have been, a surprise, she there before he was, having been round the exhibition before him and already looking on, at a table by herself but with no despondency nor that terrible negative feeling of isolation that single girls have sometimes, extinguishing all desire around them, she on the contrary a statue gazing with her living eyes at the black trees in the park. Seeing her there, yes it's her, her espresso and tobacco, nothing else on the table, staring at the trees, rigid and pale, he thinks perhaps she hasn't eaten, has a notion that she should eat, of taking care of the girl and taking charge of her nutrition, of strengthening the girl with a good square meal, suggesting that she lunch with him, feeding her to infuse strength and movement into her, but remembers that he isn't alone, impossible to eat with the girl for he's already accompanied by his faithful accompaniment, the girl will not go well with the accompaniment, once before she had come to dine with the pianist, just one evening in company and it had been a disaster, how could he forget, the way the girl hadn't for a moment managed to adapt to the usual, the way the girl had endured the accompaniment and the way, despite his efforts, the pianist had been unable to rescue her, no, it's not an option to torture the girl yet again with the imposed company of an accompaniment, nor is it an option for the pianist to be tortured from starter to dessert by his inability to fix the problem of the girl's non-adaptation to the accompaniment, impossible to sit through that, the sight of a girl like her, the image of her there from first course to last, he gives up on inviting the girl, still approaches her table and stops for a moment, Hallo salut! the pianist says, how incredible to see you here, amazing! I had no idea, hadn't a clue, dachte nicht, he's translating simultaneously, marshals his language as best he can but his eyes already elsewhere, eyes go before speech, in a flash, ein Blitzblick, out of control he plunges, through the eyes into the mouth and the back of the throat passing right under the soft palate hurtles down the trachea as far as the stomach red and shiny as a heart, right there on the thrumming stomach will diffuse like fresh blood into the artery which winds down around the leg, starting at the top of the thigh where the legs cross he starts to feel dizzy and heaves back up to the middle, here thanks to valiant exercise of reason's safeguard makes a determined effort to tear himself away, he has no business, he our pianist, in the girl's insides, time to present his excuses, his eyes make out the escape route and with a few words about the exhibition and the countryside around Neuhardenberg the words follow the eyes' example, he goes on amiably, yet driven by an unknown imperative mentions Schoenberg's Blue Self-Portrait which has particularly struck him but as if the Blue Self-Portrait were fading out behind that expression 'particularly struck' such that it no longer struck at all, ends up taking polite leave of the girl, turns and returns to his faithful accompaniment, with the ease of habit at last allows himself to be led towards a table near the great bay window, chooses a place with his back to the girl, facing the black trees. He has the idea of ordering a tall blended whisky on the rocks and is to be found shortly after, holding his glass and swirling the ice, there with his everyday company deep in vast solitude, the very kind that holds nothing for him, he'll realize that this solitude has done nothing and never will do anything for him. Better with his usual accompaniment than with the girl who understands without feminine decorum, he thinks, tries to convince himself, looks out gloomily at the black trees, this is how he should be, much better to be accompanied than understood, much

much better. He lays his jacket over the back of the chair and sits as if on a piano stool, he's never known how to lean back, wouldn't refuse to lean back if he had to but has long ago forgotten the possibility of leaning back, feels relaxed straight-backed like this, sleeves rolled up as in spring, plays his part in a laidback conversation that helps digest their guided tour of music and the Third Reich, the meal is pleasant, the food exceptional. The gleaming and beautiful trout presents to eye and knife an extraordinary flesh, the white burgundy, ideally chilled, felicitously accompanies the sweetness of life in company. At this juncture in the pleasure of his usual accompaniment the pianist mentions the Blue Self-Portrait by Schoenberg, can't he talk about anything else, a self-portrait he hardly knew anything about, discovered at the exhibition, a painting which, he says again, 'particularly struck' him, can't he say anything else, in this expression dissolving away the Blue Self-Portrait which strikes nothing at all, it's enough to call the Blue Self-Portrait a particularly striking work just once to be rid of said Blue Self-Portrait, he remarks to himself with a tacit cheerless irony, but time marches on, the pianist gives the accompaniment a sign they should leave, going back past the girl's table he will not stop again, twice would be once too many, will devote himself to the future both near and distant, the schedule that drives him, he is aware, his open-cast mine of a career, smashing the resonant ore, his career and nothing but the mineral in the open air, that weighs on him at times, rarely, like a tragic destiny.

I'm all fired up, my sister said, I saw so many things in Berlin, I heard so much music in Berlin, I got so so many replies and also came up with so so many brand-new questions that you see me now full to bursting. I've such an urge to play the violin you can't imagine. I shall jump on my violin soon as we're at the airport, I'll work like a nutter and my feet shan't touch the ground, I've a maniac energy for music, I've such an urge to work I could easily get my violin out right here in the plane, straight away, it's such torture waiting for landing. Do you think it would bother anyone if I got my violin out in here? my sister asked quite capable of doing it. My sister could play the violin in a plane, she played the recorder in front of the Bauhaus Archiv, wanted, in front of the Bauhaus Archiv entrance, to go straight into a bird-and-recorder duet and did it, played the recorder with the sole aim of holding this free public duet with bird, although without her violin but luckily with that medieval school-supply instrument shaped for collective happiness, had begun this passerine improvisation, she'd said, without sheet music or rehearsal, in front of the Bauhaus Archiv, without the least shame but with passion, moved as my sister often is, since she was little, this is how she'll behave, absence of shame—and passion. Violin she'd certainly have played if she'd had a violin with her, the recorder was better than nothing and perfect for the bird, she plays violin sitting beside the other violinists following the score and in her row, she plays in several symphony orchestras and directed by several conductors, but also plays the violin anywhere at all and when the desire takes her and directed by no one, but in the end did not get it out in the plane. I'll wait, my sister said, till we've landed because if I'm playing the violin I can't enjoy the plane to the full. Like all pilots airline pilots are nutters, said my sister, they've all blown fuses in their brains, otherwise they couldn't be airline pilots, you don't become an airline pilot by accident, you have to be completely loopy from the start to want to be a pilot, even an airline one. You've got to have quite a few screws loose to do that job now I think about it, and my sister set to thinking about what it might mean to be an airline pilot, went deep into the poetry of this technical idea. I was relieved that she'd given up on pulling out her violin, I wasn't in the mood for musical antics, I took music seriously with Adorno on one knee and Mann answering him from the other one, with the pair of them on my wobbly knees and moreover the pianist who went on making me bellow in silence, no really I wasn't in the mood to listen to my sister playing the violin on the plane. Don't imagine I had any problem with my sister, I've never had any trouble with her behavior in general or her violinist's exploits in particular, I went through the same education as my sister and recognize the same deleterious impact on her, I've adopted a lenient attitude to that education, in any case towards its effects on my sister, although I don't apply the same dose of lenience when it comes to the effects on myself. I excuse my sister everything and myself nothing, not only do I excuse without calculation but I appreciate more than anything in my sister that which I loathe more than anything in myself, I consider magnificent in my sister whatever horrifies me in myself, am unconditional with my sister and always disappointed in myself. Believed myself capable of a good hour opposite the pianist without betraying the effects of my education and succeeded only in terrorizing him with those very evident effects, to the extent that I had to leave the pianist sure that I'd put him off seeing me ever again, even by accident, instilled a lifelong revulsion in him for the kind of girl I am, the kind who talk too much and whose flaws we know well, who go on exasperating those around them down the generations, who ruin the lives of their husbands, children and lovers, never content with that understanding silence required for happiness, girls wanting so to take part in the collective happiness with their thoughtless chit-chat that they wreck every opportunity, chitting here and chatting there not stopping to count to ten, every time thinking they ought to have stopped their agile tongues and counted to ten but every time the thought comes too late. Ich habe zu viel gesprochen, I said to the pianist hoping to repair the irreparable, and for him kindly to reassure me, but no, not at all, it's quite all right, but obviously thinking it's quite the opposite, otherwise he'd never have taken me to the cinema in order to shut me up.

The pianist suggested we go see a film. I went along to

the cinema in the Sony Center, opposite the Kaiser Café. It's the perfect spot for an attack, the pianist commented in the middle of the Sony Center, walking towards the cinema, they planned this place in Berlin tailor-made for terrorism, before there was nothing here but a great piece of wasteland that the terrorists didn't even know existed and now this Sony Center exhibited here as if built to draw terrorists' attention, this symbol of capitalism replacing the wasteland where for some years hawkers of bits of wall used to scrape a living, the more wall you sell the less wall remains to sell, the trade ran out of steam and ultimately foundered due to scarcity, supply trailing demand, everyone wanted some wall to remember the wall by, there were a few big buyers, collectors who bought the best sections and framed this brand-new artistic heritage of humanity while on the wasteland market they were still scrabbling for the most insignificant pointless pebbles, nevertheless certified genuine vintage, and exposed those hawking the very tiniest pieces, hardly more than dust, until there was hardly a crumb left only flaking plaster and dust itself to sell, until the wall-hawkers had left the place, vanishing little by little, thus in a sense clearing the way for the raising of the Sony Center, symbol of capitalism, united Germany's homage to the similarly united States, the pianist was thinking about the fluctuating value of ruins in the marketplace of history. It's true that it's the perfect spot to plant a bomb, I said to the pianist with no further agenda but the sudden

impression of having understood something new about
the composer within my pianist, something that had so
far completely escaped me, understanding the composer
though too late, his inability not to be pained by this Sony
Center, not to endure it in all its capitalist splendor, was
probably driven to compose in resistance to the pressure
of the place, to compose and oppose the pressure of the
place as an individual and for all those who don't compose but keep the world turning such as it is. This is no
laughing matter, really it isn't, if this is laughter I have to
stop, I decided, I was ashamed, in the great capital's main
square, objectively the place is perfect for a bomb and
there's nothing but nothing at all that's funny about it
only this laugh would creep up on me despite the objective disaster of a bombed-out Sony Center, the drama at
the objective heart of this symbol of capitalism, a bomb
here, I don't see anything to split your sides about.
Laughing sometimes undermines commitment, particular laughter particular commitment, I could see from the
pianist's face that he wasn't suppressing a single giggle,
couldn't even imagine laughing but would quell mine
with the anti-capitalist determination of his rapid pace.
He wanted to pay for my seat, wanted to feed us, bought
popcorn, ate, I listened to him crunching the kernels one
by one right to the last, he was relaxed, the pianist in
mufti crunching away, sat deep in his armchair, it was the
moment for relaxation without a piano stool, on chairs as
on stools but in the armchair he sprawled, digging about

in the paper bag and raising handfuls to his mouth through the trailers, elbow on the armrest fulfilling the elementary function of a lever between bag and mouth, one foot resting on the other leg's thigh, he held the paper bag out to me. Here wouldn't you like some, I didn't want any but pretended to so as not to be the type who refuses, you have to know how to receive, you can't just give you also have to receive, it was a key part of my education teaching me to give as well as to receive as well as to say thank you, I said thank you a lot, it's like breathing, thanks for anything and everything, thanks for the popcorn which I didn't want but which I was happy to accept so you'd be happy, to say I stuffed myself would be overdoing it, accepted the minimum so the pianist would not lose face, took the minimum helping required for face-saving but did not take advantage of his generosity, though often I do take advantage, I mean I serve myself without restraint or consideration, I take what interests me and use it to fill my own void, my void is all I care about, I'm nothing but an empty stomach. I know because I'm personally concerned, as illustrated perfectly by my ultimately failed marriage which was intended to fill the void, a marriage I believed in for years with the sole concern of being fulfilled, that way I had of filling the marriage with all kinds of things I would bring back and cook up, my marriage was nothing but a succession of banquets of things, I told my sister in the souvenir shop, in self-interest I stocked up things and more things,

I always made a meal out of whatever it was, it all tasted good and to finish off my disgust for small dishes and for plenteous banquets and the pathological slimming. My pathological slimming marked the end of my successful marriage, I said to my sister, to sustain a successful marriage we should have kept up a desire for cooking and a desire for cleavage, not just the resources to cook out of love but also to cook for the sake of one's cleavage, so eat, said my sister and stop with the self-analysis, you need to be making red blood cells and processing iron, the analysis can come later, our priority is your blood, you need healthy blood with plenty of red and white cells, platelets and iron, for cleavage one needs aptitudes not given to every woman, healthy blood should suffice to keep your end up, no need for a belly or excess weight to maintain resistance. Take the great résistant Jean Moulin, he wasn't heavy but he had a good count of platelets, blood cells and iron, that's what made the man Jean Moulin, a varied, iron-rich diet, there is iron in strength, perhaps in popcorn too, I thought about Jean Moulin and his iron and swallowed some American cinematographic nutrition, the expression came into my head but I didn't want to say it, managed not to get started on America again, once is enough. Thanks to my capacity to accept a minimal gift of American popcorn, a capacity not innate but acquired through a successful education in the rules of exchange, further reinforced by Jean Moulin's blood, I played a discreet part in the pianist's relaxation, made his relaxation possible by giving up on all discussion of pop-corn. The results were before me, I could contemplate them despite the semi-darkness, truly fine results, courtesy of this food-sharing that I accepted knowing how to say thanks, he was, yes, the pianist in his civvies, was relaxing in the cinema. Not I. There was the problem with my legs, a long-standing problem that I've never managed to fix and which damages my social position, tarnishes my public image and makes me unfit for all cultural integra-tion. I'd be folding my legs around, crossing and uncross-ing them and hooking them onto my arms, and I'd wind up totally embarrassed by the part of myself made up of legs and this throughout the whole film, an hour and a half of leg-awkwardness, I coiled them up like venomous vipers and imagined them the limbs of a paraplegic so I'd not have to deal with them, but they wouldn't be tamed so easily, on the contrary, the more I thought about my paraplegic legs, the more alive and kicking the legs them-selves became. In the end I trapped them by wedging my feet up on the seat and wrapping the whole bundle in both arms, that's how I finished the film, in fetal position except for my head which was watching the film and not my navel. I was floating too thinking nothing but fetal thoughts but that's pure invention, I've no fetal memories and that's fine by me, I decided once again during the film: people who have their fetal memories at their finger-tips are scary, everyone who can go back upstream like salmon upriver to the spawning ground of their fetal origins terrifies me, I remembered that type, I'd never want a single fetal memory, iron-curtain out the fetal condition, that's the way to go, I'd said to my sister, that leaves space for the fetal imagination not to return to its origins in the fetal position, having no defined origin is stimulating for the memory, the quest for primal memory amounts to nothing more than dying having done nothing other than retell your founding fetal myth and nothing could matter more, I would say to all and sundry, I'd discussed it with my sister, now in the plane I was considering this discussion about origins that I'd inflicted on my sister but I could clearly see, she didn't get it, my sister and I understand each other on most things but not on origins, it's not an ideological divergence, my sister and I are almost perfectly in tune ideologically, it's a primordial and practically fundamental difference, my sister feels no drive to return to her fetal origin like salmon returning upriver because she naturally recalls her forebears and still spontaneously luxuriates in the amniotic fluid, she doesn't share my view on the original quest because she doesn't comprehend the first thing about this quest, being directly connected via her belly button to the first principles of life and knowing everything a fetus knows about the whole world, about its place in the universe and the point of ontology. My sister's expression had been forbidding, as if I were refusing her right to fetal conscience, begging me not to go on because then she'd have had to explain herself and sometimes explanation isn't possible, that's my sister, she knows where possibility ends and doesn't embark on endless discussions about the beginning of time, simply acknowledges the starting blocks for everything, not I, in the cinema I'd no way of recalling my pre-self in fetal state, all I wanted was to make peace with my legs, in fetal position and craning at the screen I couldn't follow a word of this un-subtitled American film, my English isn't good enough for me to do without subtitles and even with subtitles I wouldn't have understood a thing for I don't have enough German to follow German subtitles or only haltingly and frankly to infantile level, and even if I'd been perfectly able to understand the film I'd have understood nothing, I couldn't have got myself engrossed in it being too involved with my legs and sounds of crunching popcorn, not to mention my fundamental not-caring. I did make a few attempts to understand the film, didn't want to watch it without caring from the start, more than anything fearing this natural tendency of mine of which I'm now aware thanks to my mother-in-law that day we played our unnatural tennis match, I focused on the images applying maximum concentration in order to extract data towards a vision of the whole, did my best to appreciate the gist, envisaged the plot and intention but in the end understood nothing because of my legs and my uncaring nature which I always factor in too late. It was a spy flick with deserts and mosques, jeeps and tanks, eastern extremists and big hotels, GIs and terrorists, at the end a young man in the prime of life launched his speedboat straight at an oil tanker while praying to God, he could just as well have blown himself to smithereens in Café Einstein or the Sony Center but this was cinema. The lights went up. I was free to let go of my legs, disentangle them, to the pianist I said thanks for the film sesh, I can only see this kind of film with you, and the pianist laughed loudly, I don't know if he was being polite or if I was funny but it was true, I'd never have seen that kind of film without the pianist, I needed him so I could see it, but the film increased the distance between the pianist and me, after the tanker's final explosion I was floored, not because of the explosion though it was big enough to bring down any girl of my type, but because of the pianist's laugh. That laugh marked precisely the beginning of the end, I knew at that moment that this laughter was the very most the pianist could give me and that we would go downhill from here, from the laugh onwards I would always say too much whatever I said, even if it tickled the pianist at the time, for I'd already talked a deal too much at the Einstein and the Kaiser Café and anything I might say could never overwrite everything I'd said before but would accumulate to it, much too much said indeed even before I asked the pianist to excuse my chatter, entschuldige, ich habe zu viel gesprochen, not at all, it's quite all right the pianist had replied in French but he had nevertheless taken me to the cinema in the Sony Center.

If I hadn't been standing right by the Sony Center when he'd called this would have been a different story, I thought in the plane. The significance of the place came back to me thanks to Thomas Mann, who believed deeply in the power of time and place, of ambient conditions, as the pianist had pointed out, knowing the Manns father and son like the back of his hand, in other words knowing the Mann spirit as shared by the whole Mann family, Venice and its temporal conditions can change a man, the pianist had said during the conference at the Humboldt University, the sanatorium alters you from top to bottom, the effects of the Mediterranean and the North seas are not identical, exile in America transforms you, you're different in Davos than in Hamburg, different in Venice than in Munich, in Munich than in Zurich and in Zurich than in Pacific Palisades. Yet the pianist had not included the Sony Center in his vision, he couldn't see himself evolving positively inside this symbol of capital writ large, I understood straight away though too late. Actually he had imagined another place and so another climate, the place determines consequent conditions, he'd talked about Brecht's house, would indeed have felt much better in Brecht's house than in the Sony Center's Kaiser Café, so much better that, at the Einstein, he'd proposed our next rendezvous be at Brecht's house, to spend an evening in that house nowhere else, we could've gone for a stroll round the Dorotheenstadt cemetery which is next door, the cemetery where Brecht himself is buried, he'd suggested a little stroll in the cemetery, there's no comparison with the Sony Center, besides at no point had he thought of going for a wander in the Sony Center yet here he was against his will, nothing to do here but go to the cinema, the only place in the whole Sony Center where you can forget the Sony Center, forget both the Center and Sony the multi-national, while at Brecht's house it would be nonsense to forget the house where Brecht lived or Brecht himself and sensible rather not to forget, everything being quite charming here, Brecht's tables and chairs, Brecht's unfussy decoration, Brecht's simple garden, Helene Weigel's homely cooking which was Brecht's food, the ambiance of Brecht's cellar and the warm, intimate ambiance with Brecht smoking and drinking into the small hours, reciting poems and drawing on the tablecloth. No one would ever think of planting a bomb in Brecht's house, none of the hubris of a United States of Germany in this house. Next door you can visit the cemetery where Brecht, Helene Weigel and all their friends are buried, the pianist said, Brecht's philosopher friends, the musician friends along with the poet friends, there's a crowd of them in the cemetery, Brecht is decomposing in good company in the Dorotheenstadt where Hanns Eisler and Paul Dessau and Arnold Zweig and Heinrich Mann are also decomposing, and a great many more great minds and earlier dead and who knows who besides, the pianist here in this particularly favorable environment for composition, a place you might think entirely conceived for composition and not for consumption, a place in every way the opposite of the Sony Center, composition and consumption fundamentally incompatible, consumption decomposing quite differently than the cemetery, everything is in the manner or in the sentence object, he knows this without ever having to be taught and before learning any grammar and before writing his first German compositions, before seeing the Dorotheenstadt cemetery for the first time and then tasting Helene Weigel's cooking in Brecht's house, he knows this because it's impossible for him not to have known it since the beginning, since before his birth, he particularly appreciates the company of Eisler, Dessau and Brecht as they are here, dead and buried, has no fear of the company of this heap of corpses, appreciates advanced decomposition, well-dressed bones, shirt collars, jackets woven on Silesian looms, blue trousers made to measure in Leipzig, well-polished shoes with rusty nails, without eyes to appreciate the might of the Sony Center, without ears to suffer the ambient music of that symbol of the United States of Germany, without eyes or ears but with shoes and clothes on their bones, all six feet under, that's a good deal better than in an ashtray, ashtrays don't keep you company like the tomb, the pianist remarked in Dorotheenstadt cemetery where he often used to go not after anything directly helpful for composing, but each time noting the positive effects of the decomposition of Brecht, Dessau and Eisler, of those three particularly, on his compositions. He goes to engage with decomposition no plans for his own composition and each time is surprised afresh by these three, asks nothing of Brecht nor of Dessau nor Eisler, is not visiting them on the hunt for inspiration, yet each time leaves the cemetery in fine composing fettle, then goes to eat Helene Weigel's cooking in the cellar at Brecht's house or weather permitting in the garden at Brecht's house, but the very moment he is offered the menu with its renowned traditional Weigel dishes he suddenly feels disguised in this house of simplicity, as a pianist and not like Eisler in shirtsleeves and braces, not at ease like Eisler in Brecht's house but imprisoned in his pianist's clothes, the lost simplicity of Kurt Weill and of Brecht, a statue in the house of memory, imprisoned in the cultural institute, suddenly the Pantheon-esque scene, Brecht's decoration in the poorest of taste, Brecht's chairs notoriously uncomfortable, the Weigel menu inedible and Weill's music nothing but peasant tunes, the pianist could have done with the girl that day, that girl and no other in Brecht's house, he could have seen the girl seated on one of Brecht's simple chairs at Brecht's simple table, crossing and uncrossing her legs beneath that simple table as if beneath any table, he'd have sat opposite and they'd have had no need to come to conclusions about Brecht before arguing over not Brecht but post-Brecht, a brand-new era opening up after the death and decomposition of Brecht, that decomposition conducive to composition, an enjoyable subject in the girl's company, her breasts so barely there that you could see her breathing through them, he has an inkling that she maintains no interaction with the dead as dead people, never goes to cemeteries generally although the Dorotheenstadt cemetery is obviously different, has never knelt in contemplation at gravesides nor laid flowers on them, going to see the once-living now dead no this is not the girl's cuppa and at Dorotheenstadt she doesn't lay flowers, there's no call for flower-laying, she goes not intending to kneel or contemplate but then what is she seeking here, seeking a reason to run away as her reason to live, explores death's home as a means to escape, to run and live as far away as possible but then you really need a reason, bringing herself close to death was the only way the girl could approach the tombs and feed upon the dead. She had never dined on the dead with pleasure but always declined the dish, no thanks, had never donned black weeds nor wept in fear but had always felt chilled upon contact with it, come to this place to seek the source of the chill, hoped to set down here all the corpses she'd been carrying without realizing why the chill, how long had the girl been carrying corpses without knowing why so cold, when exactly had her will to heft run out and had she decided to set them down where they should be, carry them as far as Dorotheenstadt and once more sense close by that death she no longer wished to bear, here to let them go abandoning them among the others, then to get away as fast as she could, he saw the girl dart off down the path, her little frame in motion made him want to whisk her away with him. You have to turn away from the dead as corpses, leave the dead where they are for what they are the girl said stomping back up boyish her shoulders loosed, they're non-living that's all, not missed but well and truly gravitated into the grave, while you're right here, he would say it to the girl whose bones articulate so charmingly as she walks rapidly, almost flying, would like to say it to her, to catch her by the humerus and in one movement grasp her radius and cubitus, we're missing nothing without them but we can miss something without a live person, any person alive but you more than anyone, the dead have disappeared, the living do not disappear, always leave at least an absence which is not nothing but rather a gap, the gap when a live person disappears but a dead one you have to laugh, people who talk to the dead are lacking a bit of life but here in Dorotheenstadt talking is possible, the cadavers of Brecht and Eisler and Weigel and Dessau, we can talk to them. You can stay as long as you like before the tomb of a dead man he won't say a word that hasn't already been said, when it's said it's said and when you're dead it's too late, but not at Dorotheenstadt, dead isn't too late, the pianist rests his hand on the girl's topmost vertebrae, standing face-to-face with decomposition, meditative as if for the first time, her neck under his fingers he knows she knows, doesn't explain, Oh no never more but sees her hair flying it's a song from after the war, the street in the locks of girls gone gathering, the wind rushing in do you remember down those ravaged streets of Berlin, Oh those post-war girls just like you, no hairpins to pull out no more needles to ply, no more babies to change, the bedraggled daughters of cadavers going to scrabble under fallen stones for firewood and sparks of life, you like those girls, the pianist thinks, his fingers on her vertebrae as though on the white keys, the girl feels the virtuoso pressure on her neck, you forget everything, tomorrow same as yesterday you'll have forgotten him, he plants the chord across the white keys and makes her turn around, gently to me turn around look at me, he murmurs and smiles then, she sees his teeth, will think oh beautiful teeth, and the handsome mouth the girl thinks naturally his smile also very fine, a charming laugh between things said and those still potential, to speak and talk of the decomposition required for composition or for anything at all the main thing's the mouth, look you can count the teeth inside, and he's aware of the tongue's invitation, knows his tongue, uses it to talk of the effects of decomposition upon composition, would like to hold it for another time because what's the good, she already knows all about Dorotheenstadt, without experience but as if by magic she's understood it all, I can see you know the pianist says to the girl but please look at my mouth moving, twist your hair round your finger and untwist it, now love my teeth, not only my teeth or my mouth or the totality of the whole, these black and burning eyes my rifles trained on you, how not to crumble into flames before these pistol eyes, girls love it, and down the forehead curls fall, and over temples and neck the tumbling of hair still damp from the post-war rains, she understands of course she understands but what? The rains here don't last, says the pianist covering the girl with a section of his coat, he guides her towards Brecht's house, come little blind girl and shelter at Madame Weigel's, for she refuses to understand, nothing, understands nothing, in truth zero comprehension in the girl's silence, no point talking about decomposition with her understanding none of it, he thrilled to her incomprehension and didn't, wanted nothing to do with the girl and wanted her, the rope affects the leap, just once I'd like to break my neck. Since I was very young, here's how he justifies it, yes very young, going back to that time, whoever hasn't experienced benevolent understanding in their very earliest hours has been deprived, how does one grow up with such deprivation, with what damage, he tries to convince himself, understanding and benevolence brought together around the cradle unmissable, of course plenty of babies do miss out, the majority if you go with the stats, those babies have counted that out even before breathing their first, make do for the most part with the air they're breathing, a joy for a number of babies, actually for the great majority, growing up misunderstood and neglected, never dream of a better fate, you don't see what's missing, you have to have known benevolent understanding in order to miss it, then we'll always be missing it more or less acutely because there's never enough understanding nor enough benevolence, the babies who lack for nothing are those that never had anything and yet become someone the pianist pondered watching the girl's lungs, lungs that are easy to see because her breasts are hardly there, just enough of them to give way for breathing, just enough so you'd like to kiss them but not to nestle or shelter in them, no those breasts are not a refuge, you see the lungs take their dose of fresh air like the very first breath, no refuge here, keine Mutterbrust he tells himself in German, remembering the Mutterbrust his Mummy's bosom but what did he do next? He hears the post-war lullaby, never thought he could sleep without the song that ruled the airwaves after the war, a whisper of exile beneath the mosquito net, a narrow escape, wonders why men and the artists among them and the children within them drift their whole lives from that nostalgia of the post-war and women's scents identical to the one that rose sweaty from the twin cushions of the Mutterbrust, ash on honey, sweat on cheek to slumber here, from one bosom to the next always that understanding, the fall of the Third Reich was not enough to put a stop to the power of the Mutterbrust. The question once arisen the possible reply, due to this girl the question, the mother's answer, because he'd talked to the girl about decomposition, watching the girl look at him without benevolent understanding, he'd like to have the girl but doesn't want her, he's dying to have this girl listen to him talk about decomposition, a single enduring smile from this girl and he would have achieved an entire fresh page of the most dazzling and genuinely original music, a page for which he would never have cause to blush. He did want but didn't, for her to be here yes but at the same time no, that part of her be here but not all of her, though at the same time, yes all of her, but only in part. Not forever nor even for a long time, her here this moment but that an eternal moment, her eternally not forever but right now.

We did well to arrive late at the Deutsche Oper, my sister said, it was a pity but not so terrible. It was either catch the beginning or the end, if the beginning we'd have to skip the end, if the beginning was missed it'd be the end, I couldn't have stuck out that end right after the beginning, too much is too much, you missed the beginning on purpose, my sister guessed. No, I swore to my sister, but confessed immediately after, said yes, my yes comes easily when it's a confession, and I'm quick to confess with my sister, can't hide anything from her, it's our identical educations, she knows me by heart, also knows my not-caring, an effect of the education my sister actually shared yet which effect she was nevertheless determined to reject certainly as soon as she could babble and even, so to speak, before her conception, she knows this trait of mine though she has never called me carefree and doesn't essentially believe in my not-caring, has her own ideas about disaffection which don't correspond to my mother-in-law's, doesn't give an ounce of credence to this fact of my essential being, anyone other than my sister would have put my late arrival at the Deutsche Oper down to my not-caring, not just my mother-in-law but absolutely anyone else, not just her but all and sundry had all and sundry been brought into it, I who am never late for anything, always early for everything, who can't stand lateness under any circumstance even when justified here I am late for the Deutsche Oper, not ten minutes late nor half an hour late but late by two hours.

In the underground my sister says it must be a Freudian error, of course it is, I know the Deutsche Oper stop, I've taken this line a hundred times and I know where the Deutsche Oper is but was incapable of finding it, as if locating the Deutsche Oper was not so obviously a piece of cake, the Deutsche Oper station indicating precisely where one goes for the Deutsche Oper and no other opera house, and the Deutsche Oper never having changed location, the Deutsche Oper in front of the station Deutsche Oper never anywhere else, rooted there since forever on Bismarckstrasse which I roamed up and down nearly twenty-five years ago and roamed again fifteen years ago, up and down, with, each time I roamed it, time to locate the building that's not to be confused with that of the Theater des Westens, two separate buildings for two separate art forms, and often time to find my bearings on Bismarckstrasse thanks to this building, having taken this underground line under Bismarkstrasse a hundred times, having often got off the train at this stop, Deutsche Oper, didn't recall the start time for Tannhäuser, booked tickets,

paid for tickets for excellent seats, yet didn't remember
the time, not only didn't remember but didn't want to
be bothered about when it started, a subconscious act of
resistance, not one act in fact but two, lucky you're still allowed in in the middle of the third act. You don't owe me
a penny, I said to my sister, a bare half of Tannhäuser isn't
Tannhäuser, never mind that barely half was enough for
us. Don't think of paying me back. Half of Tannhäuser
and you don't get the effect at all, I conceded to my sister.
I know, my sister replied, that's why. I didn't ask that's why
what because my sister and I had the same education,
she guesses all my plans even those I don't know I have,
like the one of completely missing out on Wagner's effect,
his Wirkung, I translated simultaneously. I wouldn't have
missed a single second of Ligeti's String Quartet no. 1 for
the world, the fact is that I arrived at the Philharmonic
an hour early, the excellent seats I'd reserved at the
Philharmonic were occupied from the first movement onwards by my sister and I whereas those, equally excellent,
reserved at the Deutsche Oper were only occupied by us
after the interval and only so to speak to the minimum,
Wagner frightens me, I told my sister, I shrink from the
Wirkung, I always put it off. That said I don't really know
Wagner, nor Ligeti really, being busy with the buttress-
ing of my soon-to-be failed marriage I had renounced
both former and latter, given up on any relationship
with Wagner as with Ligeti, given up as it turned out all
extra-marital relationships, whether with the former or

the latter or with anyone else, hadn't the first notion of a potential relationship with Wagner or Ligeti, occupied myself day after day with the fortification of this marriage to the de facto exclusion of music, chamber or otherwise, you keep up the odd extra-marital relationship at the start and then less and less, the first to go are the furthest away then little by little, the nearest and dearest too, now and then you remember the first ones then forget the very existence even of the most recent, to forget is not to recognize, I don't recognize anything, I was thinking on the steps inside the underground, anything about music whether close-up or far away so recognize nothing of Tannhäuser which I nevertheless claim to know, playing tricks on myself and missing the overture which I don't recognize but which I used to once. I did know the overture I told my sister, why of course, my sister said, you knew it, Papa always listened to the overture while he was alive, when Papa was alive, do you remember how alive he was in his car, Papa, conducting the overture with his right hand and steering with his left, how could I forget, it's fresh as day my sister said, and nothing will ever stop us remembering that, Papa and the Tannhäuser overture, first Papa and us and the overture, not Tannhäuser here or there, neither at the Deutsche Oper nor the Staatsoper but as conducted by Papa, way back when, when he was living life to the full, remember, he was living to the full by daybreak already, don't get your knickers in a twist, my sister said who never lets anyone tweak hers, but I went on getting them twisted, I judge Wagner by his reputation but not Ligeti, Wagner's Wirkung makes me afraid of Wagner, Ligeti's doesn't put me off Ligeti, and yet I booked those tickets for Tannhäuser with the sole aim of undergoing Wagner's famous Wirkung, indeed I wanted to feel the famous effect generally known as Wirkung, a transformation not an effect, at the Deutsche Oper which isn't Bayreuth but still more suited to Wagner than Papa's old banger, to undergo the Wirkung pure, unmediated and without preparation must be possible at the Deutsche Oper, yet I'd only partly experienced it due to lateness. Well played said my sister just as I was thinking it.

Crouched in the semi-darkness of the upper circle, second row, for we couldn't hope to attain our excellent seats before the interval without sparking a major contra-Wagnerian incident, I was struggling with the handle of my Woolworths plastic bag which I couldn't get off my wrist, each attempt at disentanglement of Woolworths from my person producing a horrifying storm of plastic-bag rustle, I had to wait for the brass to come in to disengage my wrist millimeter by millimeter, luckily, I considered, it's not a Mozart divertimento, I was simultaneously attempting to undergo the full Wagnerian impact in the least calculated and most immediate way, tried to allow myself to be intimately moved by the Leitmotif, almost managed it but not quite, occasionally I was pretty sure, trying to feel the full unmitigated Wagnerian effect, there, that's it, that's the true-blue Wagnerian effect, but with

these words in my head could hear myself thinking them
and that in itself created a severe anti-Wagnerian distanc-
ing to be thinking about the Wagnerian effect even while
undergoing it. I tried to think of myself as a cow, given
my musical affinity with cows since the notorious nocturnal bellowing which had even surprised me in my car and
somewhat frightened me, I thought the Wagnerian effect
on a cow would be Wagner's effect in its purest condition,
that Wagner's music and the cow's lowing might have
something in common perhaps surprise or alarm and that
the cow was therefore the animal most able to understand
Tannhäuser, that an audience entirely made up of cattle
at the Deutsche Oper, a herd of cattle all recently parted
from their calves and gathered in the Deutsche Oper
would have made the best possible audience, for no single
cow would have been trying to feel Wagner's effect nor
have sated themselves with the famous Wagnerian effect,
rather the cattle in general and each individual cow would
have undergone the full Wagnerian effect without having
a single thought on the subject, whereas the Deutsche
Oper's audience naturally had a much more problematic
experience of Tannhäuser, an experience packed full of
intelligence no matter how sensitive and stuffed with a
wealth of Wagnerian musical references rendering direct
sense experience impossible. However absurdly diminu-
tive the claims of human intelligence, it is always to a
greater or lesser extent human, I concluded still trying to
shed my own humanity. I finally managed to detach my

wrist from the Woolworths bag, a first step, now I needed to slough off all human thoughts and replace them with bovine thoughts, the setting is appropriate, I felt, noting the papier-mâché castle, the backcloth of mountains and sky and the choir done up in medieval garb, here we were fairly gone rural and perfectly accessible to a cow, the castle is a castle, the mountains mountains, the sky a sky, medieval times medieval times, a rabbit would have got it so a cow quite as well as a rabbit, this is a set equally suited to rodents as to ruminants, I've almost managed bovinely to submit to the Wagnerian effect when my sister who's a violinist, not only a violinist but a musician, leaned up to my almost-cow ear to complain about the awful flute which was buggering up every one of her entrances, that flautist should be sacked, said my sister, better Tannhäuser without a single flute than that flute in Tannhäuser, it's unreal a flute so out of tune, she said in my ear with such disgust that the humanity sitting nearby reacted with a show of perfectly intelligible annoyance, the human public was less bothered by that bugger of a flute than by your remark on the flute's buggering up, I whispered to my sister who shrugged, I'm right, my sister said, and the audience is wrong. I get a huge kick out of my sister's capacity for fearlessly stating that she's right when she's right and also for blamelessly pointing out that the audience is wrong when it's wrong. This incredible facility my sister has for asserting she's right and the rest are wrong is what I most like about my sister, truly it's the very essence of my sister, not once has my sister compromised in her determination to have right on her side even in opposition to the audience, she's never been a victim of the education for collective happiness which she has nevertheless shared with me yet which never had the effect on her that it has always had on me. From judging once more there in the Deutsche Oper, at the exact moment when I was stupidly about to transform myself into a cow, not that the animal is stupid but the transformation would be, treating the Opera House as a cowshed was all right for the Third Reich, I was just beginning to consider this when my sister's capacity for never giving in brought me up short without, however, returning me to my initial human state which I couldn't guarantee was 100 percent stupidity-free but that's not the issue at hand. Neither kine nor human, I floated in a state between, I was trying not to hear the flute but the flute was all I could hear, was trying to hear Tannhäuser despite the flute but could hear nothing but that flute buggering up, and through the flute-playing not the flute itself but my sister's revulsion, she alone with right on her side no matter the cost and that all sent me to the depths of despond. Every time my sister's education looks like a failure, my own education seems to me some horrifying success story and I slide into a state of melancholy.

No sign of melancholy about the pianist when he again mentioned the Auditorium audience, briefly mentioned, mentioned fleetingly, briefly because we were in the Café Einstein and it was by way of a rejoinder to me but fleetingly also because it wasn't in the least important, fleeting as a butterfly he recalled the audience's reaction, I still haven't understood their reaction, the pianist said smiling, he'd handled the reaction well, had been booed and hissed, had provoked scandal in the Auditorium not only as the pianist but also as a composer, had bowed to his booing audience, shaken the conductor's hand and congratulated the players and bowed again, then left the stage in a deluge of boos as if it were applause, I in the audience already sick at the thought of the pianist's feelings and also identifying with the audience and dying of shame, identifying with the pianist and dying of humiliation, he not dying of anything and leaving the stage as if to applause, not upset but reassured, indifferent neither to the boos nor the hisses but encouraged to continue on his own path. The audience didn't understand, the pianist decided, they simply didn't listen, composing a piece with the sole aim of pleasing my audience was not my intention either, would have been impossible, would have meant selling my soul as a composer, would've put an end to my life as a composer, not only as a composer but as a pianist too, and not only as a pianist but as a man even, so the pianist on returning to his dressing room and his life's work as a man, a grand statement for me but the only one that's worthwhile. Alone in his dressing room he told himself, man to man, I've written nothing of which I could be ashamed. This is how one becomes a man alone, he realized, standing before the great mirror opposite the Bösendorfer, looked unsentimentally at this incidental portrait and saw himself alone and handsome on the other side, just as he had always hoped to be. Later he'd discussed, it was evening on his birthday, fleeting as a butterfly, deep in conversation with the evening's accompaniment, the Auditorium audience's reaction, he'd never before encountered such a hostile reaction, had been even more shocked by their reaction having had faith, he added, in that audience, would never have expected such mediocrity of that audience, had almost expected something over and above ordinary applause, a firestorm of applause, not that he'd ever depended in any way on weather phenomena to seal his choice to compose but because his music, he knew, was the spirit of resistance, that this spirit of resistance was indeed, in his conception, the spirit which could best figure this city and therefore the people of this city therefore the audience not in general but of this Auditorium in particular he'd imagined as made up of sons and daughters of first-generation Résistants. The daughters and sons wouldn't only have appreciated his music because it was announced in the program as "music of resistance" but would have sought, and found because they sought, the resistance in the music, in the structure of the piece, in its compositional technique, its instrumentation, in its form and heart. Instead of which he had been booed and hissed by the regular patrons who being sons and daughters of first-wave non-Résistants weren't as a rule in the least bothered about resistance in general or by the Résistance in particular and had no education other than education in non-resistance. They're all yea-sayers, Jasager he translated, a bunch of Jasager. Now the usual accompaniment had gone up to the pianist and taken his hands, incredibly relaxed hands while the rest of the pianist's body except those two extremities was stiffer than a stiff, had kissed the palm of one then traced from there along the beloved forearm then up to the shoulder beloved likewise, embraced the pianist and taken the pianist like a baby into her arms, had soothed the baby with such right and benevolent words. Beethoven and Wagner and Schoenberg were booed and hissed so many times you can consider this experience a mark of honor, the accompaniment murmured into the composer's ear then stroked the composer's hair, the composer's neck, kissed his neck then kissed the whole of the composer, inserted her leg between the composer's legs, and finally made love to the composer. Laid out on his back with the accompaniment moving gently harmoniously tenderly elegantly upon him and without haste, he on his back hands behind his head then hands on the accompaniment's hips both of them eyes on the ceiling, letting the accompaniment ride and letting himself be overtaken by this emotion without acceleration was no easy hack as the accompaniment understood perfectly doing her amazon

turn so lightly as to be barely there, he had these three
initials in his head, BWS, no idea why the initials and
not the full names, BWS in historical order not alphabeti-
cal, he closed his eyes because the accompaniment was
probably picturing herself making love to BWS but was
only making love to him who was neither B nor W nor
S but himself, the concern came to him that if he'd been
himself alone unassociated with BWS, alone being booed
and hissed, without antecedents neither B nor W nor S
nor anyone else, the accompaniment wouldn't now be on
top of him, moving with such terrifying benevolence and
understanding. He closed his eyes so as not to disappoint
the accompaniment who was making love so well to B,
to W and to S at the same time as to him who was only
himself and not the other three, couldn't find the courage to make the accompaniment get down without this
hurtful dissonance resolved, absented himself like this,
in a muddled pleasure, in order not to contradict any of
that sexually embarrassing musical lineage. I went over
and over all the possible explanations but I didn't hit on
anything, said the composer the accompaniment now
descended and he extended, having a smoke in bed for
once, knowing that for once the accompaniment wouldn't
object, would keep quiet about smoking on account of B,
of W and of S who were still floating in the bedroom
air like figures of immortality. Hit on what? the usual accompaniment asked in her tiny husky after-sex voice. The

reason for that reaction from the audience, the composer said again not wanting to specify but repeating it anyway. Their reactionary mindset, the accompaniment replied, turning out the bedside light, abandoning the composer in that negative and unproductive solitude that was no good for him, abandoning him but keeping one arm laid over his chest. He had to wait for the accompaniment to fall asleep before he could gently free himself from this habitual arm, one mustn't assume a presence because of an arm or a leg left behind, the pianist knows. This is how one becomes a man alone, the pianist realized, not going to sleep. The Blue Self-Portrait hung on the wall, the hum of contemporaries behind the wall. Ahead of the wall the West, behind the East, if one not the other, you had to choose, Deutsche Oper or Staatsoper you had to choose, Café Einstein or Brecht's house you had to make a call, one side of the Spree or the other, downriver or upriver, now things are better we can choose but actually no we can't, between Berlin and Berlin there's no choice, you can generally tell the difference between Berlin and Berlin but not always, it gets harder, really there's no difference any more.

I have to go for a pee, said my sister, first-class at piss, a pee in front of the Reichstag and behind the Brandenburg gates, a pee in the Tiergarten, a pee at the Sony Center, a pee in Nikolaiviertel, in front of the Bauhaus Archiv a piss and at the Philharmonic, at the Deutsche Oper, on the Kurfürstenstrasse, on the Unter den Linden avenue pee in front of the Bellevue again and there right away without waiting in the rain on the bank of the Spree just after the little bridge the need takes her so there she goes, but not at the Nationalgalerie no, the only place where my sister has not pissed although I have, it was an hour before the Kaiser Café in the Sony Center, I went to pee in the Nationalgalerie, went into the Nationalgalerie specially for that not to see the exhibition about melancholy. Look it's the exhibition, I said to my sister in front of the Nationalgalerie, we could go and see it, yes we could, my sister replied who had a melancholy tendency. The exhibition had been at the Grand Palais before sprouting anew at the Nationalgalerie, I had walked past the Grand Palais and thought melancholy, hm, why not go see that but I'd let it go, every day putting it off to the next, walking past the Grand Palais, melancholy tomorrow, thought I must go see the melancholy but had put everything off while swearing I wouldn't miss it, I put it off every time so that in the end I missed the melancholy I was just too late, once over it's over, on balance relieved to have missed it, having practically forgotten melancholy and even forgotten having missed it yet now I'm here brutally confronted with melancholy in the beating heart of Berlin, a stone's throw from the Philharmonic, practically next door to the Staatsbibliothek and not much further from the Sony Center where waiting for me though I didn't yet know it was my tragic destiny, confronted once more with the decision of going or not going, the possibility of a detour via melancholy before facing the tragic destiny crossed my mind, look there's that exhibition from the Grand Palais at the Nationalgalerie, I said to my sister, so the question of melancholy reared its head again when I thought I'd decided it once and for all by dint of my apathy which almost instantly made an enthusiasm for melancholy seem vulgar and laughable. No step was taken, no commitment on my part either directly or from afar in favor of melancholy but a vague impulse, one at least, hardly framed before it was demolished by the apathy, but here in Berlin a fresh chance to bear out my good intentions, we could go I said to my sister but instead of joining the queue for tickets I snuck straight off to the Nationalgalerie toilets, the basement ones, actually not just for a pee, I'm better at holding on than my sister, but to change my Eleganti hold-ups. For a good half-hour my left stocking had been showing signs of weakness and for the last fifteen minutes had no traction on my leg at all, slithering down to a crumple, first a millimeter-by-millimeter creep then a more rapid centimeter-by-centimeter and finally in one go from the top of my thigh to my knee, forcing me to bend at almost every step to pull it up again, hoicking my Elegantis up the whole time while continuing to walk towards the Sony Center instead of heading to Brecht's house, restricting me to a hobble not only unnatural but also thoroughly ridiculous, to the extent that my need for a change of Eleganti was a good deal more urgent than that for a piss. Luckily I'd found a Woolworths

on Friedrichstrasse where I bought a new pair of Elegantis
and some souvenirs from Berlin for those who can't remember it because they weren't here, I shan't ever forget
it, on seeing the Nationalgalerie my first thought was not
of the melancholy exhibition but of the Nationalgalerie's
toilets and I didn't waste a second before heading straight
to the basement, going down for no melancholy reason
but entirely focused on resolving my hold-up situation.
Was, in a way, forced to visit the Nationalgalerie toilets
instead of choosing to visit the exhibition on melancholy,
we'll go another time, I said to my sister who while waiting for me had already begun to descend into melancholy,
had instinctively got herself in the mood, don't go down,
I said to her and snatched my sister's arm before melancholy could suck her into its depths, literally snatched her
from the jaws of melancholy, no time, come on, I said to
my sister, there's nothing here for us because I know my
sister, she and I had the same education, everything that
runs through my sister tends to run through me too like
this taste for melancholy and our fascination for what lies
deepest. Come on, I'd already said to my sister, there's
nothing for us here, that day my sister was not in the least
radiant but clung to my arm, dangled from me, was
wholly supported by me who ought to have shone at her
side that day, I'd literally snatched my sister away from
melancholy, led my sister back to the family home before
the body was carried to the cemetery and each of us had
thrown our handful of gravel on top and pronounced our

last goodbyes too late but for oneself one last pointless time, for my sister it was enough to see the coffin, Papa inside it and the candles on top, enough for her to hear Fauré's Requiem, not Verdi's, much more of a laugh than Fauré's, that one really gets you plumbing the depths and keeps you at rock bottom from the first note through to the last, come on I'd said to my sister, leaving the church ahead of everyone else and leaving Papa stuck there behind us, the two of us leaving together arm in arm and singing happy songs all the way home, you couldn't have found happier ones, listen to this, I said to my sister, it's Charles Trenet no one's ever done happier, Y a d'la joie is nothing beside N'y pensez pas trop, I was singing N'y pensez pas trop to my sister who was hardly thinking at all by now, she'd started to go back over this day of Papa's burial, decomposition recomposes us one way or another, the pianist might one day have explained to the girl, that was in Brecht's house, you have to go through decomposition in order to regain composure and face everyone again, everyone else provides the raw materials for composition, what's left isn't the unnecessary but precisely what's needed, what's left after decomposition is the raw material of composure, and that composition consists of reconciling what's left, she was in practically the same state as Papa the day of the funeral but she revived while he didn't, I held the spoon to my sister's lips, one spoonful for Papa, one for Maman, one for you, I sang Trenet to my sister and set her back on her feet, made her do easy little walks in the garden until she was fit to take her violin out of its case, to hold the violin under her chin and herself against it, and to start to revive by playing, leaving the Nationalgalerie my sister was walking in the evening sun and glowing in the luminous decline, water has flowed under the bridges declared my sister who can read my mind, we can breathe more freely here, I was breathing in the fresh air, walking towards my tragic destiny on the arm of my sister who was also breathing, never twice in the same river, once is enough, that's how it was I saw the tragedy ahead, no comedy of repetition in the tragic, we keep going and that's all. I kept going with my plastic Woolworths bag in my hand and my sister on my arm towards the Sony Center and not to Brecht's house, tragically towards the Sony Center, going on and that was all, leaving the Philharmonic on the left and the Staatsbibliothek on the right, my left and my right I've never been sure of them but I'm guessing that the hand which holds her arm is the right one which is it seems the more important hand but only from one point of view, guess where I am, my sister said to her phone, guess! Outside the Philharmonic! Imagine, me right here, in front of the Philharmonic! she was glowing lit up by the setting sun which was sinking behind the point of the Philharmonic while I was walking tragically towards the Sony Center, declining towards the center, I'm going back to the B&B my sister was saying to her phone, I'm leaving my sister in good company, I'll have a drink with her first, fire her up and remind her how she's really worth it, she's worth a lot, an awful lot, under-estimating her is bad for the exchange rate so I aim for inflation, I big her up and I leave her in good company, she's waiting for the pianist to call, she's head over heels for him, my sister said, she's in pieces, I'm not going to leave her in pieces and arse about face, I'll raise her exchange rate and then she'll be on a level playing field with the pianist, I'll wait for her at the B&B, leave her in that inflated state and get busy with my violin, I'll play in my room in this little Polish B&B, I'm going to work at it like a madwoman, I'm itching to play the violin, I have to play, it's the last evening before we fly, just this evening left and tomorrow we're off. Tonight Berlin and tomorrow Paris, we'll come back, we're going but we'll come back.

Inside the Kaiser Café my sister left me to await the arrival of my fine company and gave me her parting tips, you are not intellect alone my sister, think of your body, think of straightening out your legs, try to untangle them and drop your shoulders, you have to relax, one day we'll go to a Turkish bath, think of the Turkish bath, she left and I dived for the first time into the correspondence, Lieber Dr Adorno on one side, Lieber und verehrter Herr Dr Mann on the other, trying not to expect too much of our meeting, to expect as little as possible, preparing already to expect nothing ever again, staking everything on the correspondence, burying myself in it to the point of disappearing altogether, Lieber Dr Adorno on one hand, understanding nothing fundamentally but plunging, able only to drown to swim you have to have learned and to learn you have to have dived in, plunged in the correspondence, Lieber und verehrter Herr Dr Mann on the other hand, when the pianist made his entrance. I saw the pianist enter and I knew he wouldn't save me from drowning but would press his pianist's hand on my head and clap his lovely pianist's hand over this mouth of a girl who's said too much already but perseveres, not straight away no first he'd watch me struggle but then he'd do it, he'd help me to disappear, would press that hand down and apply that fine hand and would make me shut up, shut up the pianist would say pushing my head down his hand clapped over my mouth, shut up now don't say a word stop talking, don't say a single word either in German or French or in any language please shut up, you have to shut up now, there you go, silence, the sooner the better, I had very little time before the head pushed down and the hand clapped over, I didn't know how long but very little. What was I really after, I wondered, why did I want to talk to this pianist, not to converse with the pianist or shoot the breeze but to go to the heart of the matter before being reduced to silence by the pianist's two hands, go for broke, as if he'd asked me for the crux of it whereas obviously he hadn't, had no interest in what mattered that particular day rather preferred to avoid it, was pursuing quite other ends, life is infested with matter what use is talking about it, he looks straight ahead, the strasse des 17 Juni leads to the Brandenburg Gate and behind it Pariserplatz, go round the roundabout, several times round for thinking time, could be anywhere but is here going round and round wondering how he can solve the problem of the Blue Self-Portrait, its musical composition like the painting's composition, its composition a re-composition without imitation or plagiarism but aligned with the painting up until that end for the beginning is superb, truly superb, he's sure of it, the best beginning he has ever come up with, he's managed some decent ones and even some excellent but this beginning surpasses anything he'd ever thought possible, the crucial matter exposed right from the start, its inadequacy already in the first phrase, the bare essence, the black trees of Neuhardenberg figured by the entanglement of signifying lines, the interplay of timbres and the singularity of this polyphony whose further developments he'd been able to arrange like spiky branches, yes it's the spitting image of the Blue Self-Portrait, my self-portrait like Schoenberg's, you had to hear this opening of the Self-Portrait with full orchestra, at the piano already brand-new and already on the staves original yet still faithful to the first idea, faithful thus to the original without plagiarizing the original nor acting as an allegory or evocation or metaphor, its fidelity outside and beyond the original, and yet you could never dream up anything closer to the original, so much so that listening to this opening you are immediately in the presence of the painting, this the usual accompaniment had confirmed having seen the Blue Self-Portrait by Schoenberg then heard the opening of the Blue Self-Portrait by the pianist and compared the one to the other, had reassured him it's a good opening, reassured a very good opening, but had not begun by calling it an excellent opening, only a good opening, the composer hadn't believed her, this wasn't a good opening or even a very good opening it was in point of fact an excellent opening, he knew it and wasn't really relying on the accompaniment to confirm the truth about the opening being certain the opening was excellent but the finish still a limbo, the middle perfectly good, the middle in keeping with the black trees and the exhibition in the background, he had rendered that background by a violent turn to tonality, the twelve tones and then a sudden drop into tonality, got hold there of a genuine idea which nevertheless came only to partial conclusion amid the upper-octave distortions of the prepared piano, the usual accompaniment had heard the end but made no distinction, judged the end as she did the beginning, had reassured him about the end, it's very good the ac-companiment had said but obviously that wasn't true, the accompaniment could easily have said excellent but he knew it wasn't, had no illusions about the end's weakness and could not leave the end as he'd first imagined it, so thinly imagined, an end that wasn't really an end but a conclusion without urgency, a procedure whose end was, an expected end, in line with the audience's expectations, forming a certain unity as it were but in fact a betrayal, a traitorous end, that's what I've composed, an end imagined without imagination, imagination the power behind images, no power and no images in that end, no power hence no image, no image hence no power, the absence of imagination in this end would bother no one but myself, no one would be disturbed by this lack of imagination in the shape of image-forming power, no one if not myself, the end absorbed as easily by our audience of regular patrons as by the accompaniment, all applauding the end, no one challenging, no one taking a stand against this unworthy final procedure, this unheeded betrayal bothering absolutely no one apart from me who would betray myself with this ending.

No one but myself may decide my end, breathed the composer slowly as he drove in the setting sun, crossing the bridge over the Spree, passing the Philharmonic and re-entering the underground car park, with this realization he felt in no way empowered, rather lost once more in the negative solitude that did him no good, no one but myself, lowering the window to take the ticket, he would have liked someone beside him in the car, a girl perhaps who would tell him what she thought of his end, thinking no one but myself alone in the car is not the same as saying no one but myself to someone, a girl like that girl who would cross and uncross, who'd twist her hair round her fingers and would of course know not to say anything about the end as she knew that no one but he, she would understand the end's shortcomings without benevolence but as if by magic. Enclosed in the car with him on the third level below ground of the Sony Center's car park, she would listen to that end, not the end by the painter-composer who finished his portrait having left out an ear, but the pianist-composer's end who was finishing a piece that demanded full attention from both ears, she would understand straight away without a word about the end nor with any kind of comment the inadequacy of this end, of course, the girl would say, the end needs another go, not the very last notes the girl would have said but the finish, the finish rather than the very end, in fact it's the scherzo the composer realizes, that provocative inversion into tragic mode in the scherzo demands a finish, not a conclusion, no one but I, her apart, that girl, knows better than anyone except me, mind if I smoke? asks the composer and the girl makes a rollie for him, they stay there smoking in the car and now perhaps he understands, teenage-parked in here with her and the contained curls of smoke, the idea he'd been missing, musical, for the finish, to finish the piece in that volatile, intangible way, drop that obvious rallentando that trips too naturally into the G-flat to B-F-D-flat triplet sequence, pick up the initial theme in the right hand but no brio at all here, from the D-flat the chord this time in inversion, sing the inversion to the girl, invert the girl, invite the girl to come back with him and invert her at his place, in his Berlin apartment while the accompaniment is out, not inverting the girl on

the bed but running his fingers all over the girl like a teen-
ager and letting her fingers touch first here and then
there, touching first a bit then a lot then endlessly, waltz-
ing endlessly in the apartment with the girl in a waltz
that's so slow no idea why so slow and losing his balance
with her and imagining her dancing with no one else ever
again, alone with her dancing, no one else ever, squeezing
the girl in his arms but without lifting the girl, letting himself spin floating turning slowly and floating slowly, letting
himself go with her in that so-slow waltz, he knows the
impossibility of romantic love, which has no resolution
except in death that he knows of, let's get out of here not
stay where we are come to my place says the pianist gear-
ing into reverse, come to my place another time, if you
like, the next time you're in Berlin you can stay at mine,
there's space here, my accompaniment's offspring has a
room here but she's not around much, you could have the
offspring's room if you wanted, next time, when you're
back in Berlin. Thanks, I said to the pianist, that's very
kind but no, to take the accompaniment's offspring's
room unmöglich, not something I can countenance,
spending even one night in the offspring's bed would
mean dying in that bed, would mean quite simply killing
myself in the bed, would obviously mean giving up all
possibility of getting up again, I'll never survive, said it
not joking, of course I'm exaggerating and I'd have survived like the cow survives the disappearance of her calf,
her last-born like the ones before, would have mooed for

two or three days straight then survived and finally gone
on living day after day and season after season, would
have thought of it then not much then not at all, exaggeration along with not-caring my salient features, another way of putting two fingers up at the world, staying
carefree in the offspring's room is however much more
imaginable than staying there and hoping to die, as if it
were so important where a girl sleeps, here or there, one
room or another in the end what difference does it make,
thanks but, all in all, I prefer a little Polish B&B on Neue
Kantsrasse to the accompaniment's offspring's bedroom
in your apartment, I nevertheless replied with as much
nonchalance as exaggeration, because the little Polish
B&B is not objectively preferable, nonetheless among the
shabbiest and sorriest, the black forest freeze emanating
from the B&B staff, sleeping in a Polish forest or sleeping
in the B&B on Neue Kantstrasse is six and half a dozen,
the chill and the darkness and fear of wolves and the winter solitude, the tapestry in room 203, the deer in the
tapestry, the Polish state of the electrical wiring, the Polish
condition of the bed-linen, the Polish room service, I
pictured the accompaniment's face at having to put up
with me in her offspring's room so near the pianist and
having to put up with me in fact everywhere in the apartment, I as always incapable of respecting hospitality's
limits and overstepping them at the first opportunity and
at all those that follow, by my omnipresent presence de-
stroying an environment propitious to well-conceived

conjugality, the quiet and benevolent friendly complicity of conjugality when it's genuinely shared, my big mouth talking too much from sparrow's fart, even before breakfast I'm motoring on and without thinking to spread the marmalade on my Brötchen I plunge in, in my typical scholarly, passionate and extravagant fashion, like that from my first words of the day, from the moment I first open my mouth and as if to compensate the tooth I'm missing, already before morning coffee is done I'll have talked too much, in my passionate and triumphal and candid, shameless fashion, Maman did not teach me modesty certainly not, I said to my sister, we can't blame her you can't think of everything, we'll have to make the best of our education, I said, our education wasn't the worst either, went on, still we can't blame Maman nor Papa who followed Maman, peace be with him he went straight to heaven like a man of nature, of wild nature, not beautiful nature, of wild woods not of gardens à la française, we can't blame either one or the other for this dreadful education, they did their best, didn't educate us so badly in the end, I look at us and I know there's worse, that day I was optimistic and said to my sister who wasn't at her best since Papa was dead and she wasn't yet, that yes, shamelessness is a basic handicap but not the worst, that of course shamelessness sabotages us, makes us misfits and more arm-bombs than arm candy, that of course education for collective happiness makes us unresistant and fundamentally influenceable by the best and much more often by the worst, but see, my sister, what nice girls we are, really very nice girls, Maman did not screw that up and Papa neither, dead his soul at peace having at least succeeded in making truly nice girls of us, very very nice. As nice as us is very rare, as fundamentally is exceptional, I said to my sister who didn't see why, for my sister being nice is so natural she doesn't see it, thinks everyone is like her, doesn't know, doesn't see the nasty on one side and nor the nice on the other, imagines everyone equally nice, no villainy or perversity but a universal niceness. Collective happiness, in my sister's case, depends neither on satisfaction nor on abnegation but fundamentally on universal niceness, the one does not preclude the other, my sister said, it's due to excessive niceness that I've found myself in the most immodest situations, stripped bare by niceness and soon fetched up in a strip from which I have only emerged thanks to the niceness of others, niceness has never prevented shamelessness in my case, to be honest my niceness has much more often fed my shamelessness such that for me niceness has always been a disaster. For me but not you, I replied because I've never believed in disaster striking my sister. Others may believe that, not I, I've heard tales about her, the acres burned down in her wake, the suicides and nervous breakdowns, the despair of artists who've painted her portrait, the demolitions of façades and crumblings of cliffs which speak volumes

about my sister's capacity to provoke, my sister's provoca-
tions have been a feature of her whole career, although
never catastrophic for her, my sister emerges a hero from
all misadventures thanks to her non-stick character and
to a stubbornness that I call perseverance, misfit and
arm-bomb are compliments to my sister while both being
appalling flaws in me, declining the pianist's invitation is
yet another symptom of my antisocial character, the pianist will of course have observed, the lack of elementary
politeness in this categorical refusal is due to my unclub-
bable character, saying I preferred a Polish B&B on Neue
Kantstrasse to the offspring's room in his apartment is
proof if any required that misfit and arm-bomb are, right
after carefree, the terms that best describe me, which the
pianist will have noticed, no longer risking an invitation
except to the cinema in the Sony Center, invitation to
which I responded positively. If you like we could go to
the cinema, the pianist said in French out of politeness
and love of the language and I said ja warum nicht.

You had to hear me say that warum nicht to the pianist, a warum nicht at the Kaiser Café is not a warum
nicht at Brecht's house, there is in that Kaiser Café warum
nicht a readiness for suicide that the same warum nicht
at Brecht's house could never convey, Kurt Weill's music
and Helene Weigel's food are essentially suicide inhibi-
tors, the pianist had said to all who would listen, Weill fills
us with life and Weigel's food likewise, not with that lively,
joyous life singing in the open air and collective life as

life can be in a way, but with a life that resists collective, singing, joyous life, there are limits to the joyous life the pianist had said to all who would listen. If, in Brecht's house, I had been invited by the pianist to sleep in the offspring's bedroom I'd have said a warum nicht of resistance so nourished by Helene Weigel and by Kurt Weill, but nourished by nobody at the Kaiser Café I spoke that collaborationist and suicidal warum nicht, why I didn't say to the pianist that I'd nevertheless prefer to sleep in the offspring's room than go to the Sony Center's cinema I don't know, though actually I'd much much much rather have ended up in that tiny room or rather roomette with the pianist than in the Sony Center's cinema, and would probably have preferred to find myself in the roomette even without the pianist than at the cinema with him, would've preferred the roomette to room 203 at the Polish B&B, yet I said no to the roomette and yes to the cinema, I'd really like to understand, I told my sister. You are able to say no for tomorrow but not today, you can say no to an uncertain future but not on the spot, no in general yes but no in particular no, that's how you are, I know because you and I are the same, my sister said in the plane, identical educations, saying yes is good but not no, you have to say yes Maman used to say having always said yes in general down the generations which made her say no in particular, used to say you mustn't say this or that, no, above all don't say that, used also to say you mustn't do this or that, above all don't do that so I'd say

yes to Maman as a general yes while my sister who said
yes was thinking no, I obedient but she disobedient, that's
how my sister has been from her very first yell, my sister's
waah still ringing in the maternal ears but my absence
of yelling all the more, we can't hear her, I would hear
people saying about me, obedience doesn't make a fuss,
I thought in the plane, at the same time as my sister was
remembering her yes that had nothing in common with
any obedient yes, my own yes always so servile but my sister's yes always free, she remembered she'd always say yes
too soon, I always say yes and then regret it, sometimes
I even regret it before I speak and knowing I'll say it like
the day I got married, my sister said, I can't swear to it
but I do think I started to regret it before I said it but said
it anyway, because I'm contrary. I've also said it anyway,
I told my sister, but I don't know why, I've said no but too
late, when the choice was irretrievably limited to no or
no such that my no lost all meaning, choosing no or no
is easy, as the guide said in the Musée de la Résistance et
de la Déportation, saying no in particular when the yes is
general, yes, the guide was saying, the no of those names
up there is a more resistant no than the no of the names
that followed and which aren't written up because they
don't deserve the name of Résistants, first- and second-
wave are not the same, the guide explained, first-wave
are the first and the second wasn't too late but as good as,
and as good as too late is well and truly too late. It isn't
always possible to say no, the guide said as we reached

Déportation, sometimes no is quite simply impossible to say but possible to think and sometimes even impossible to think, but also not, either.

After his concert in Lyon, a concert of resistance for which he had composed resistant music, not just composed but interpreted its resistance at the piano, a general resistance but also specifically to Lyon, the pianist had decided to see the exhibition and followed the guide through the rooms commemorating the deported and begun to consider the Jasager, he who says yes. The question of Ja or Nein appears to the pianist not a new question but an old one, a very old, ancestral question, the Jasager's ancestors whom we're obliged to deal with, doing deals with the ancestral Jasagers is an ongoing business. Composing a Neinsager would be one way of not giving in to the yes, the pianist thought; he had decided to talk about the Jasager in the Musée de la Résistance et de la Déportation's lecture hall specifically in the presence of a communication specialist, i.e. a specialist on Jasagung, on communication in the Resistance as everywhere else and on the piano in communication as on Resistance and Deportation in communication, the communicant was asking the pianist questions about music and the Resistance and the pianist answering the communicant, the pianist sitting beside the Jasager was seeking an escape route, caught sight of the fire extinguisher, choosing not extinction but exit, saying yes to say no and not no for no, no for yes but not yes for yes, the extinguisher is no for no the exit yes for no, ultimately in the dark was hunting for his escape route. She was there. Sitting not on a folding seat but perched on the steps. He looked at the perched girl, saw nothing beyond the girl yes her alone, legs crossed and uncrossed and hair around her finger twisted then untwisted, now to leave the plateau of Resistance and go into hiding, to abandon the Jasager and abduct the girl, come now, I've an hour before the plane, just one no more, no time to resist you any longer, don't tremble the pianist said, took her by the waist oh minuscule waist in the pianist's hand, come follow me don't speak whatever you do don't say a word don't be afraid I shan't do anything to upset you, nothing I swear we're just going to walk to the bridge and on the bridge you'll see the river just that and you'll have that particular air coming off the water to breathe, the air will rise off the water up to you and in the air if you like I'll kiss you the French way, leaving the Gestapo HQ transformed into a museum and with his hand around, beyond believing, his hand around her, the girl's waist so slim it was unbelievable, couldn't get over her waist and dared not move his hand away, the pianist's hand keeping her feet on the ground, with my hand here on her surface I'm keeping her on the ground and among the living, she is so light the pianist considers the air off the river would be enough to lift her, a squall not required to carry off the girl, a mere flux of river air and she'd be gone; he stops in the middle of the bridge, he is standing above the water, what to talk about now between the Gestapo and the

airport, the girl's hair hides her face from him, he reaches
out, brushes the hair away, leaves his hand in her hair
and the other hand, the one from her waist, moves to her
neck, and up to her cheek her temple and the forehead
of the motionless girl who doesn't see the green river, she
sees only me the pianist knows, me that's all, I fill her
vision now and moves closer to the girl and kisses the
girl, kissing her would make her die the pianist knows but
kisses again and dying over again, don't move don't say
anything not a word nothing please be quiet the pianist
says and kisses her again and infinitely on the bridge like
that above the river, no thought of the future, suspended
together eternally above the river as if after Goethe neither Flaubert nor Beckett had followed it's funny to think,
as if after Beethoven there'd been neither Wagner nor
Schoenberg and yet he lets go, a pianist can't play with his
hand clenched, has always inscribed his hand in time and
inscribed music in the gesture and the gesture in time,
music without time is an imposture the pianist knows,
he knows his departure time, doesn't look at his watch,
sand can't be gripped in a fist, has never missed a flight,
takes off at the pre-ordained hour every time but on this
bridge with the girl how not to stay forever, a little of that
slight gold still held between his fingers, once more please
the pianist says, küss mich noch einmal, he is young
Werther, won't wait for her reply and mingles oh yes his
tongue with the girl's which doesn't respond as a usual
accompaniment's would, responds without motherliness

or understanding but in way that's so strange it's almost savage, not violently savage but strange and naturally savage, which is to say not cultural, no trace of culture in this girl's tongue, nothing to suggest any command of culture, wholly uncultured from head to toe, this is what drives the pianist completely crazy, intolerable ignorance, stop! the pianist says to her, hör jetzt auf! bitte hör auf! repeats at the girl but actually to himself, and she then not asking why because she knows without having learned it and as if by magic, parts her tongue from the pianist's tongue and parts the pianist's hand from the nub of compressed sand and his other hand from her neck and fingers from her cheek, ear from his eyes, the substance from the form and the parts from the whole, goes on her way completely parted onto the western bank, as if by magic goes away on the other side of the bridge, doesn't look back just goes, so it goes, in the realm of Resistance, thinks the pianist and as if it were important, thinks this not vaguely but in these precise words as if to be written in a private notebook, ridicule does not kill, quite the contrary.

We don't know why, on leaving the bridge by the eastern side, the idea first came to the pianist here of a self-portrait, a portrait of a man alone and handsome, alone but not destroyed, the solitude of the composer, atonality as an abstraction, abstraction as an isolation, isolation as a resistance to the world, the world as unacceptable reality, impossible to make peace with reality, aware of the day as of the time and returning to the Gestapo HQ he would learn through the composition of this self-portrait, would understand through the self-portrait the refusal to compromise in composition, saying this in front of the Gestapo he found the cultural group he had left behind there and the Jasager, the group leader is always a yea-sayer, follows them into the Gestapo to drink a last beer with the Jasager and his aggregation, last drink before the airport, in the Gestapo's little drawing room with this restrained group that is, the pianist realizes, the Jasager's accompaniment, but in the Gestapo lounge waiting for his last minutes to pass, he was already writing the first bars of the Self-Portrait, inventing by unknown technique a minor-key atonality is this imaginable around F-sharp, could clearly see minor atonality anchored around F-sharp, a bit of good fun, this called for an allegro in so-nata form without a true second subject, then descending via D-flat a scherzo veering into scherzando, the comedy of the Self-Portrait suggested it, the isolation of the comi-cal dispatched by, why not, a Beethoven-style pedal effect, and as if inverted, a comical, burlesque self-portrait, we'd be in the river here, he considers a green shade but for this portrait seeks a more negative color, one colder than cold, the correspondence of colors and sounds an idea to follow among the feathers and squawks of nature but also into the science of cultural confusion, this idea of a muddled science that's always producing images without light, performances without audience, pure and fantasti-cal abstraction, the chill of colors and the chill of sounds, considers a correspondence around F-sharp, this F-sharp turning slowly into E-flat, had time to write none of it here, was trying to hold on to the key ideas even while drinking to the Resistance in the Gestapo HQ, drinking a toast with the Jasager, distractedly finishing because composing elsewhere and already on the plane.

We're still airborne but lower and lower said my sister, feel how we're lowering, we're beginning the descent, I'd say we've turned south-west, my sister said again who has a sense of direction, I don't, I've never known my right from my left never mind the points of the compass, my sister does though, has always had a sense of direction never been wrong about a route except when being contrary but otherwise never, knows all the possible trajectories in advance, knows where they go and never questions them while I do, one route or another most of the time I don't see the difference or much too late, in my car bellowing on the road, I don't know which road, know nothing about that road except it was twisty and there was snow on it and I used to take it every day in the days of my apparently reasonably solid marriage which was actually already a total failure, going up and coming back down every day the same route to get away from my failed marriage as I headed down and believing as I came back up in my successful marriage, going down with the hope of not coming back and coming back up with the hope of one day going down without the hope of not coming back up, going down with a desire to live and

coming back up wishing I could die, going down to live
and returning to die, then one day going down to avoid
dying, which I did in fact manage, I said to my sister, not
only managed not to die but managed to come back to
life, that's the very minimum, I managed that minimum,
almost didn't make it, just made it, my sister said I know.
I know you off by heart, you think you're doing the minimum when actually you're always doing the maximum,
that's what my sister was saying, and your maximum is
not everyone else's maximum but an exceptionally lofty
maximum, my sister said, your maximum is fearful to
behold, that's why you need to eat well and sleep well
every day and every night, you need to be taking care of
yourself my dear, she was betting on health, saw in well-
being the only way in general and for me in particular,
begin with short outdoor walks, I know you like walking
and nature when it's untamed, my sister said, you can't be
counted on to cycle or get into jogging or go to the gym
but outdoor walks are what works for you so start there,
my thing would be Turkish baths, rather, yours is outdoor
walks, remember you once saved me with a nature walk
my sister said, walking up as far as the oak and coming
back down again was enough to revive me remember, my
sister said, sometimes that's all you need, Kant went for
outdoor walks, Bergson too and Schoenberg took constitutionals and Thomas Mann went for walks and Proust
too was into walking, Papa took them, said my sister who
knew Kant and Schoenberg and Mann and Proust and

Papa very well and thinks I know them too because my sister and I had this shared education which makes my sister expect we'll have shared affinities, my sister has a habit of forgetting that in my case this successful education has rendered me unfit for Kant and for Bergson, unfit for Schoenberg as well as for Thomas Mann, Proust and Papa, even though failure in her case opened the door to all of Kant and all of Bergson and all of Schoenberg and all of Mann and all of Proust as well as all of Papa, I didn't dispute it though because I really like how my sister believes that like her I'm completely free to discover the constitutionals of inspiring great men and to envisage this incredible synthesis of great men's constitutionals in general and of these men's in particular, synthesis I'd never have thought of myself, I need my sister to believe in my admiration for great men, my sister's admiration for great men is equal to her knowledge of great men while mine is on a level with my ignorance.

I admire you, I'd told the pianist no joke in the corridors of the Auditorium and remembering that now as we came in to land made me scream there and then soundlessly as a cow might perhaps scream soundlessly when after a few days her calf is not there, scream without calling for it knows perfectly well where to draw the line, already screaming no longer in hope but with death in its cow's soul, is apparently grazing peacefully as if no calf never carried one nor gave birth nor fed nor loved in its instinctive cow way but thinks of it screaming as I was thinking while silent screaming that I'd said to the pianist unlaughing that I admired him, which was entirely false, I swear on my sister's life which is much dearer to me than my own life: I've never admired the pianist. I really think I said I admire you to him solely in order to test the effect admiration might have on the pianist and as a kind of kamikaze operation, for his violent disappointment was patently visible, the pianist stopped mid-declamatory flow, brutally cut short, a stop put to his continued declamation by means of my declaration, his eyes emptied of all positive expectation, entirely filled with negative disappointment, I'd have liked to tell him, but couldn't tell him, as I had thought to myself while saying I admire you, that it was for a laugh, that I didn't actually believe in admiration and didn't in fact admire anyone as a rule nor pianists in particular nor this one among them all but was truth be told unfit for admiration, I'm not fit to admire great men, admiring Kant and Bergson and Schoenberg, same with Mann, Proust and even Papa is not something I can do, yet I said I admire you that day to the pianist, I did wonder why seeing the pianist's face and his disappointment, because I really didn't admire him and had no intention of admiring him nor any likelihood of finding admiration in a future either near or far but I said it and when something's said it's said, I put it down to my suicidal education in collective happiness and have torn my hair out over this education which is always catching up with me, actually it arrives before me, I blamed my education but not my mother or my father who have nothing to do with it, I recalled in the plane, they managed to make a nice girl out of me, it's pretty rare to get as nice as me never mind my sister. What I like about myself, I said to my sister who was watching the earth's approach through the porthole, is that I'm a nice girl, and you too such a nice girl. I know my sister said and I knew she knew for she knows everything I like about her and about myself, as nice as us is exceptional, I was saying while shivering hot and cold all over, everything all at once, this flaw is our best flaw, I also said to persuade myself, niceness should not prevent us from being inventors of air brakes, my sister'd lamented, I'd really love to have invented them myself air brakes but I was much too nice, between air brakes and niceness the line is you have to choose, I'd've had to stop being nice to do air brakes, I tried but I didn't succeed, if I've one regret it's having failed with air brakes, will you look at that handsome invention, an invention such as the air brake makes my head spin, the pianist could equally have invented it, that air brake, I said, he had everything going for him from the start, instead of which he makes do with playing the piano, but he could have done it too, not that he's a bad person either, nothing bad in the pianist and absolutely everything non-bad but non-bad isn't nice you follow. Of course I follow, my sister said although she couldn't actually see the difference between being non-bad and being nice because she thinks absolutely everyone is nice.

I didn't feel like explaining my ideas on nice and non-bad to my sister, it wouldn't have done my sister any good to change her world vision according to my notions of the nice and the non-bad, every aspect of my sister's vision is all right by me because it works for her, one's world vision can be a great and beautiful thing I thought as we went on flying although much lower, a great and beautiful thing when it's my sister's but otherwise not, if not hers a world vision would be better smaller-scale than so big, Weltanschauung I translated automatically and that took me straight back to Tannhäuser, I felt a chill rising through my legs and running under Adorno on one side and under Mann on the other, each warming the blood and returning the blood to me at about the right temperature by the time it flooded my thumping heart which has nothing to do with the open heart of heartiness, heartiness is found not in the beating heart but in the one that is disciplined, far from the blood and screams of a cow on losing its calf. The vision of Tannhäuser destroyed by the cow's desperate love for its calf, this was a total Weltanschauung which rather screwed me up and by means of a recreated instant screwed up the time of the cow, which truly does see each second's dying.

Weltanschauung is not one of the pianist's words, it's absent from the pianist's vocabulary, I'd recognized and understood the pianist's hostile stance to all Weltanschauung from the start and even before he conceived it, when the pianist came across the Blue Self-Portrait he really fell

hard for the intentional absence of Weltanschauung in
Schoenberg's canvas, in which rather than both his ears
the painter depicted just the one. For Schoenberg one ear
is enough the pianist had observed and understood, the
intensity of a single ear is the extent of what's useful for
Schoenberg, the pianist struck by the absence of the other
ear and wondering, understanding, the whispers of contemporaries was enough for Schoenberg, two ears for a
whisper is obviously far too many, a single one pressed to a
wall enables better audition of contemporaries than two,
one ear is enough to listen and two to confuse the whisper
with noise and the noise with clamor and the clamor with
the terror of undergoing collective Weltanschauung, the
single missing ear, the ear missing an ear cut off and all the
missing and cut-off ears, humanity no different from the
cornered bull, ears mutilated so as to hear only the crucial
whispers and not the clamor, mutilated and tossed in a
heap like a pile of shoes is tossed, we could have avoided
the heap of shoes by making the choice, as Schoenberg
did, of a single ear, the other blood and phosphor organ
wrapped in the linen, solo blue ear the one listening to his
contemporaries, the pianist thought as he left the Sony
Center car park, could only with the girl and never another have talked about that single ear and whispered in
the girl's a music for contemporaries, the contemporaries
who, the pianist had said in the Museum of Resistance
and Deportation, are the sons and daughters of the shoe-
thieves, the shoes of children and the elderly alike, the

contemporaries the sons and daughters of those who didn't stop them, said the pianist, to the audience and not to the girl, she from the top of the steps had understood perfectly as she would have understood perfectly in the Neuhardenberg Castle restaurant, and heard which is to say understood too in the car the opening whisper of the composer's Blue Self-Portrait, a polyphony of disjointed timbres, he'd have whispered in the girl's ear now lying beneath the black trees, the girl shivering again but with desire, don't speak be quiet please don't say anything shut up the pianist began again where he'd left off, listen please, in the natural last-of-winter silence not yet the joyful spring of migrating birds, our contemporaries' whispers, this piece is the only music worthy of you, this piece is for you, listen it says nothing about the world as a whole but whispers a limited knowledge of the world, for you a limited and partial knowledge keep listening, would have slowed the heartbeat his and the girl's and lost himself in the girl, could have lost himself in that listening, would have lost control of the music in the girl's ear and stripped the girl bare beneath the black trees emptied of migrating birds, and dressed the girl in his brand-new composition, he wouldn't merely have heard but heard with sympathy, would have lost himself beneath the black trees and close to the end, his body now lumpen and numb as before decomposition, stiff except for his hands, still he tries to be close to a body, not the girl's but the body reading by the bedside light, the familiar almost family body of a usual accompaniment, tries to recover the serenity of what's his in body and mind, would like to return to the calm warmth of the usual accompaniment's Mutterbrust but senses in alarm a tepidity that chills him. "That I have written nothing I should be ashamed of forms the foundation of my moral existence" hears the supine pianist and sees again the Blue Self-Portrait on the wall, Schoenberg with his one blue ear frightens him when the usual accompaniment reads propped on her elbow, soundless but for slow and peaceful and terribly warm breathing, the odorous, heavy, anti-musical breathing that crashes over the pianist's ear like a barbarous buzzing while beneath the black trees, his ear upon the girl's ribcage, he was memorizing for ever the ever varied and imaginative and genuinely original breathing of the girl, exact echo of the whisper, that I've written nothing, moral existence, written nothing, existence, morale, written, moral, existence or nothing, was not falling asleep.

Sleep a bit, if only, close eyes to sleep and not to think or pray or feel but yes sleep, oh to sleep at last! here now without thinking much about it yet without struggle or striving, I closed my eyes but no more than a few seconds, sleeping in planes is impossible beside my sister whose delight in flying does not let up before landing. There's Paris can you see, my sister said, we're insanely lucky to see Paris from this particular spot in the sky, I once flew over Paris in a helicopter it was unforgettable but from here look and it's Paris with the river, different from the

plane than from the helicopter, Revoir Paris my sister
sang Un p'tit séjour d'un mois, Charles Trenet always
and over again since the day of Papa's funeral, the day
of my sister's resurrection and Papa's both at once, my
sister's resurrection ought to have restored Papa and not
the other way round, seeing her resplendent above Paris I
realize once again, seeing my sister's splendor is generally
enough to bring anyone to life but our father in particular
certainly, as for the other way round we'll have no idea
right up to the Last Judgment and even then not sure.
Papa would have loved to see this, my sister said reading
my thoughts before I'd thought them, that's so her, to say
simply Papa would have loved this, yes I said, this more
than anything, flying in the plane and seeing the river
and Paris all around the river from here like us and also
seeing my sister and I so nice each of us and each to the
other, I could kill myself thinking how much he'd've loved
it, Papa, seeing this, the incredible panorama us in the
plane and Paris down below, nothing to anyone else but
everything to him, his pride seeing us in the European
sky no hatred for anyone and so nice, the great war he
never experienced rubbed clean away and the other one
that messed up his childhood, both wound up and us
two flying there, my sister afraid of nothing and without
a word to say against anyone and I seeing Paris forgetting as the cow forgets her calf, forgetting the language.
Thomas Mann and Theodor W Adorno slipped from my
still-weak knees and fell closed over each other beneath

the seat in front, I picked them both up and stowed them together in my bag. The plane descending the language moves on, German fades out, I can already feel it fading out, I said to my sister, it does this every time, an hour and a half for German to fade right away, I've nothing more to say I who talks too much, have no language left only the music and in the music alone the escape routes, that's a good sign, I said to my sister, forgetting the language is a beginning. My sister knew before I said it, she's just like me, precisely the same although not, I'll fit the pieces back together, there, I'll take some time at home quietly fitting my pieces back and I'll eat well and sleep well, I'll take outdoor walks, that's what I'll do, I said to my sister, I too shall be radiant. You will be radiant my sister said my sister, from the moment we reach the airport you'll start to feel different and as though you're glowing, the plane isn't as good for you as for me I can see that, flying only makes you melancholy but you'll see once we're back on land. Look, land! Land!

The captain talked the standard talk about outside temperature and the few minutes that remained of the descent, eighteen degrees the captain said with pride, it's definitely warming up, the pianist began to get dressed. From his veranda he had watched summertime take over the Tiergarten, how the decision to change season was ratified by the trees, the sky and the city suits, light clothing, Parisian elegance, to go for a stroll, yes walk now, go for this stroll in the midst of the new climate which has plucked him from his faithful night, streaking the sheet with this ray of random particles which seemed to fall directly from the wings of an angel. He'd go as far as the angel, would cross lawns with the first of the wild rabbits and begin to make out his ending, walking like this on the soft grass would conceive a reprise, a return to the allegro in sonata form without a true second subject, after the inversion have the torrents of birds come in around the G, to swoop down as far as D-flat and there, suspended, silence, nine beats, plucked strings, diminished fifth followed by the cluster describing a chromatic circle from where he will draw, through slow, low-pitched contiguity, the pure negativity of the blue. He would stop in the midst of the rabbits because, despite the planes passing overhead and the blackbirds' clowning, he'd hear yesterday's anxiety thickened with weakness and regret which would, in this new dawn of time, make him feel right to the tips of his still fingers that chill sensation, the chill that never left the girl, that girl no other, then, as if it was funny, he would stare at the green trees and, shading his eyes with his hand, would salute the just-flown figure of the Blue Self-Portrait.

Translator's Note

INSOUCIANT: are we ever, enough, too much?

Funny that one of the keys to this novel should be not caring. Our heroine is castigated repeatedly, and repeatedly berates herself, for the crime of "désinvolture." What is this elegant French notion? Why, nonchalance, insouciance, of course. Plain old frivolity, laidbackness, devilmaycareism, happy-go-lucky style; in the plainest of English, it's not caring. But she does care—hence all the obsessing—and, as my narrator's translator, so must I. Funny then how impossible it was to find the right single word to translate this term so often reiterated it counts more as a musical leitmotif than a point of prose argument. I considered all the words above at one time or another. Also flippancy, apathy, heedlessness and casualness. I swung between the light and breezy, désinvolture as a delighted freedom from the burdens of the world, and désinvolture as culpably turned-off, disaffected, absent. None of these was precisely wrong. Their problem was irremediable specificity, where Lefebvre's magisterial word said them all and more in one go. After discussion and disagreement that lasted some months, my editor and I came to near-agreement on the one term that said nearly as much as the original French: "not-caring" (occasionally, a more standard "not caring" too, depending).

In addition to saying as much as we could make it say, the plainness of "not-caring" and its verging on neologism seemed appropriate, for Lefebvre's language is often about language, and also languages. *Blue Self-Portrait* plays out in a French sown through with German and English, American English mostly. The narrator herself is frequently on auto-translate, trying herself out in different languages, over and over, back and forth. Our plain-Englishism belies the history of French, English and more behind it.

Important too, for this term and many others in the book—accompaniment, counter-phrase, nice and niceness, shame and shamelessness, legs knotted and unknotted, overviews of waterways, criticisms of cars, cows' lowing, flute-playing, so many more—is the very twentieth-century musicality of their use, the repeated striking of these notes in ways that recall the leitmotif we imagine as we listen to twelve-tone music. Remember (Lefebvre doesn't let us forget; in her book forgetting is another highly culpable error) that our Blue Self-Portrait is first of all a genuine painting by the seminal twentieth-century composer Arnold Schoenberg, who invented the twelve-tone serial system and thereby enabled classical music to become a truly modern and modernist art form. As Lefebvre probes how we can remember some of the most shameful ideas of the last century, she weaves her text in approximation of a serialist piece. Not only had I as translator to find the right note or word to strike, I had also to strike it as nearly as possible every time Lefebvre did. I was expecting this translation to be a tough job and so it proved.

Nonetheless, I hope your experience as reader is at least as much of a giggle as it is a serious interrogation of your attitude to history or a test of your musical antennae. No, I hope it's more a giggle than anything else, for Lefebvre's dominant key is absurdity. Translating this girl who imagines herself as a cow mooing loudly enough to break the glass in her plane's portholes, a girl who despite hang-ups gives as good as she gets to her one-time mother-in-law over a tennis match, who delights in her parachutist's boyfriend's irreverence and can't rein in her neuroses even on dates with her buttoned-up "world-class" pianist love interest, has been a hoot, if an unexpectedly educational one.

Sophie Lewis
January 2017

NOÉMI LEFEBVRE was born in 1964 in Caen, and now lives in Lyon, France. She is the author of three novels, all of which have garnered intense critical success: her debut novel *L'Autoportrait bleu* (2009), *L'état des sentiment à l'âge adulte* (2012), and *L'enfance politique* (2015).

SOPHIE LEWIS is a literary editor and translator from French and Portuguese into English. She has translated Stendhal, Jules Verne, Marcel Aymé, Violette Leduc, Emmanuelle Pagano, and João Gilberto Noll, among others.

Transit Books is a nonprofit publisher of international and American literature, based in Oakland, California. Founded in 2015, Transit Books is committed to the discovery and promotion of enduring works that carry readers across borders and communities. Visit us online to learn more about our forthcoming titles, events, and opportunities to support our mission.

TRANSITBOOKS.ORG